t

The King's Gold

The King's Gold

Arturo Pérez-Reverte

Translated from the Spanish by
Margaret Jull Costa

W F HOWES LTD

This large print edition published in 2008 by
W F Howes Ltd
Unit 4, Rearsby Business Park, Gaddesby Lane,
Rearsby, Leicester LE7 4YH

1 3 5 7 9 10 8 6 4 2

First published in the United Kingdom in 2008
by Weidenfeld & Nicolson

A CIP catalogue record for this book is available
from the British Library

ISBN 978 1 40741 484 3

Typeset by Palimpsest Book Production Limited,
Grangemouth, Stirlingshire
Printed and bound in Great Britain
by MPG Books Ltd, Bodmin, Cornwall.

FSC
Mixed Sources
Product group from well-managed
forests and other controlled sources
Cert no. SGS-COC-2953
www.fsc.org
© 1996 Forest Stewardship Council

To Antonio Cardenal
for ten years of friendship,
films and fencing

What do we gain from it all? A little glory?
Some rich rewards, or merely boredom?
You'll find out if you read our story.

Garcilaso de la Vega

CHAPTER 1

THE HANGED MEN OF CÁDIZ

The reason we are brought so low is that those who should honour us instead conspire against us. Once, it was enough merely to brandish the word "Spaniard" for all to tremble; now, for our sins, that reputation is almost lost . . .'

I closed the book and looked where everyone else was looking. After several hours without a breath of wind, the *Jesús Nazareno* was finally heading into the bay, driven by the westerly breeze that now filled the creaking mainsail. Grouped along the deck of the galleon in the shadow of the great sails, soldiers and sailors alike were pointing at the corpses of the English, which either adorned the walls of Santa Catalina castle or hung from gallows erected on the shore along the boundary of the vineyards that faced out to sea. The bodies resembled bunches of grapes ripe for harvesting, except that these grapes had been harvested already.

'Curs,' growled Curro Garrote, spitting into the sea.

He had greasy, grimy skin, as did we all: soap and water were in scarce supply on board, and

1

after the five-week voyage from Dunkirk via Lisbon bringing home the soldiers from the war in Flanders, the lice were the size of chickpeas. Garrote bitterly stroked his left arm, rendered almost useless by the English at Terheyden, and gazed in satisfaction at the San Sebastián sandbank, where, opposite the chapel built next to the lighthouse, lay the smoking remains of a ship that the Earl of Leicester himself had ordered to be burned, with as many of his own dead on board as he could find, before re-embarking on another ship and fleeing with those who had survived.

'They paid a heavy price,' someone said.

'And would have paid a heavier one still,' said Garrote, 'if we'd got here in time.'

He would gladly have strung up some of those bunches of grapes himself. The English and the Dutch, as smug and arrogant as ever, had attacked Cádiz the week before with one hundred and fifty warships and ten thousand men, determined to sack the city, set fire to our ships in the bay and seize the treasure fleet that was due to arrive from Brazil and New Spain. In his play *The Girl with the Pitcher*, the great Lope de Vega began his famous sonnet thus:

The Englishman bold, armed only with trickery,
Thinking the lion of Spain asleep in his lair . . .

And that was precisely how the Earl of Leicester had arrived, the typical cunning, cruel, piratical

Englishman – however much the people of that nation may hide behind privileges and hypocrisy. He had disembarked a great many soldiers and succeeded in taking the fort of Puntal. At the time neither the young Charles I nor his minister Buckingham had forgiven the rebuff received when the former had wanted to marry a Spanish infanta, who kept him waiting around in Madrid for so long that he finally lost patience and returned to London with his tail between his legs. I'm referring to the episode, which I'm sure you'll remember, when Captain Alatriste and Gualterio Malatesta came within an ace of putting a hole in the young King's doublet. However, unlike the day thirty years before when Cádiz was plundered by the Earl of Essex, God chose otherwise this time: our men were armed and ready, the defence was hard fought, and the Duke of Fernandina's soldiers were joined by the inhabitants of Chiclana, Medina Sidonia and Vejer, as well as by any infantrymen, horses and old soldiers who happened to be to hand. And thus we Spanish gave the English a sound drubbing, and the English hindered our efforts only by spilling a great deal of their own blood. After much suffering and having advanced not one inch, Leicester hurriedly re-embarked when he realised that what he could see heaving into view was not the treasure fleet but our galleons: six large ships and a few smaller vessels, Spanish and Portuguese – for at the time, thanks to the great King Philip's inheritance from his

3

mother, Spain and Portugal shared both empire and enemies – each one equipped with good artillery, and carrying veterans coming home on leave and infantrymen from now disbanded regiments, all of them battle-hardened from the war in Flanders. When our admiral had been given the news in Lisbon, he had set off for Cádiz under full sail.

The heretics' sails, however, were now nothing but tiny white dots on the horizon. We had passed them at a distance the previous evening as they limped home after their failed attempt to repeat their good fortune of 1596, when all Cádiz burned and when they had plundered even the libraries. It's amusing how the English make such a fuss about the defeat of what they, with heavy irony, refer to as our Invincible Armada, and about Essex and so on, but they never mention the occasions on which they came off worse. Poor Spain may have been an empire in decline, with more than enough enemies eager to mop up the sauce with their bread, but the old lion still had teeth and claws enough to go down fighting before its lifeless body was shared out amongst the crows and the merchants. They, duplicitous Lutherans and Anglicans all – Devil take 'em – never had any problem combining their worship of a very indulgent God with piracy and profit – among heretics, being a thief had become one of the respected liberal arts. If one were to believe their chroniclers, we Spaniards made war and enslaved people purely out of pride, greed and fanaticism, while those who murmured about us behind our backs – they of course plundered and trafficked and exterminated in the name of liberty, justice and progress. But that, alas, is the way of the world. What the English left behind them on this occasion was thirty ships lost at Cádiz, many colours brought low and a large number of dead on land – about a thousand, not counting the stragglers and drunks whom our men mercilessly hanged from the city walls and from the gallows erected in the vineyards. This time their plan blew up in their faces, the whoresons.

Beyond the forts and the vineyards we could see the city with its white houses and turrets tall as watchtowers. As we rounded the bastion of San Felipe and the port finally came into view, we could already scent the earth of Spain the way donkeys can scent grass. A few salvos of cannon greeted us, and the bronze mouths protruding from our gunports offered a loud response. At the prow of the *Jesús Nazareno*, the sailors were preparing to drop anchor, but only when the men had scrambled up the yardarms to take in the sails, and the canvas was flapping loose on the spars, did I put away my copy of *Guzmán de Alfarache* – bought by Captain Alatriste in Antwerp as reading matter for the voyage – and rejoin my master and his comrades on the forecastle. Almost everyone was excited and glad to be once more within reach of land, knowing that all the troubles of the voyage would soon be over: the danger of being hurled onto rocks by contrary winds, the stench of life below decks, the vomiting, the damp, the meagre daily ration of rank water, the dried beans and the worm-eaten ship's biscuits. A soldier's lot may be a wretched one on land, but it is far worse at sea. If God had intended man to live there, he would have given us fins, not hands and feet.

When I reached Diego Alatriste's side, he gave a slight smile and placed one hand on my shoulder. He looked thoughtful, his green eyes studying the scene before him, and I remember thinking that his was not the expression one might expect on the face of someone arriving home.

'Well, here we are again, my boy.'

He said this in a strange resigned tone, as if being here were no different from being anywhere else. I, meanwhile, was gazing ahead at Cádiz, fascinated by the play of light on its white houses and the majesty of its vast blue-green expanse of bay, a light so very different from that of my birth-place, Oñate, and yet which I also felt to be mine.

'Spain,' murmured Curro Garrote. He sneered as he said this, pronouncing the word as if he were spitting it out. 'The ungrateful old bitch,' he added.

He touched his shattered arm again, as if in response to a sudden pang of pain or as if he were trying to remember why it was that he had been prepared to risk both limb and life at Terheyden. He was about to say something else, but Alatriste shot him a stern glance with those piercing eyes of his, which, along with his aquiline nose and bristling moustache, gave him the threatening air of a cruel, dangerous falcon. Alatriste looked at him briefly, then at me, before once again turning his cold eyes on Garrote, who said nothing more.

The sailors had dropped anchor, and our ship stood motionless in the bay. Black smoke from the fort of Puntal still hung over the strip of sand that joins Cádiz to the mainland, but the city had otherwise barely been touched by the battle. People had gathered near the royal warehouses and the customs house and were standing on the shore waving, while feluccas and other smaller boats gathered round us, their crews cheering as if we had been the ones to drive the English from Cádiz. Later, I learned that they had mistaken us for the advance party of the Indies fleet, whose yearly arrival we, like the soundly beaten Earl of Leicester and his Anglican pirates, had anticipated by a matter of days.

And God knows, our voyage too had been long and full of incident, especially as far as I was concerned, for this was my first experience of those cold northern seas. From Dunkirk in a convoy of seven galleons – with various merchant ships and Basque and Flemish privateers bringing our numbers up to seventeen – we broke through the Dutch blockade as we headed north, where no one was expecting us, and fell upon the Dutch herring fleet, of whom we made short work, before continuing round Scotland and Ireland and returning south across the ocean. The merchant ships and one of the galleons had left us – at Vigo and at Lisbon respectively – while the larger ships sailed on down to Cádiz. As for the privateers, they stayed in the north, prowling the English coast and doing an excellent job of plundering, burning and generally disrupting the enemy's maritime activities, just as they regularly did to us in the Antilles and wherever else they could. Well, God willing, what's good for the goose . . .

It was on this voyage that I witnessed my first naval battle. We had sailed through the channel between Scotland and the Shetland Islands a few leagues west of an island called Foul – a black inhospitable place, like all those grey-skied isles – when we came upon a large flotilla of the herring boats the Dutch call *buizen*, under escort by four Lutheran men-of-war, amongst them an *urca*, a large impressive storeship. The merchant vessels with us stood aside, keeping well to windward, while the Basque and Flemish privateers fell like vultures on the fishing boats, and our flagship, the *Virgen del Azogue*, led the rest of us into battle against the Dutch men-of-war. As usual, the heretics made excellent use of their artillery, firing on us from a distance with their forty-pound cannon and their culverins, all thanks to the skilful manoeuvrings of their crews, so much better adapted to the sea than the Spanish. This was a skill in which – as the disaster of the Great Armada demonstrated – the English and the Dutch always had the advantage, for their sovereigns and their governments encouraged the nautical sciences, took good care of their sailors and paid them well, whereas Spain, whose vast empire depended on the sea, merely turned its back on the problem, accustomed to giving more importance to the soldier than to the sailor. Indeed at a time when even common port prostitutes boasted aristocratic names like Guzmán and Mendoza and the army still felt that it had something of the nobility about it, the navy continued to be considered one of the lowlier professions. The result was that while the enemy had plenty of good artillerymen, skilled crews and captains experienced at sea and at war, we – despite our excellent admirals and pilots and even better ships – had only valiant infantrymen. At the time, though, we Spaniards were greatly feared when it came to hand-to-hand fighting, and for that reason during naval battles the Dutch and the English usually tried to keep us at a distance, to dismast our ships with cannon shot and batter us into submission by slaughtering as many men on deck as possible, while we struggled to get close enough to board, for that was where the Spanish infantry was at its best and had proved itself to be both ruthless and unbeatable.

So it was during the battle near the isle of Foul, with us as usual trying to edge in closer, and the enemy, as was their way, trying to prevent us from doing so with almost continuous fire. Despite this onslaught – which brought down half the rigging and left the deck awash with blood – the *Azogue*, managed valiantly to get in amongst the heretics, so close to the Dutch flagship that we actually rammed their forecastle with our spritsail. From there, grappling irons were thrown, and a horde of Spanish infantrymen boarded, amidst much musket fire and brandishing of pikes and axes. Not long afterwards, we on the *Jesús Nazareno*, now sailing to leeward and firing on the enemy with our harquebuses, saw that our fellow Spaniards had reached the quarterdeck of the Dutch flagship and were brutally repaying the enemy for what they had hurled at us from afar. I need only say that the most fortunate amongst the heretics were those who jumped into the icy water to avoid having their throats cut. Thus we captured two men-of-war and sank a third; a fourth, badly damaged, managed to escape, while the privateers – for our Catholic Flemings from Dunkirk did not hold back – gleefully plundered and burned twenty-two herring boats, which desperately tacked this way and that, like chickens trying to outrun a fox that has sneaked into the chicken run. And at nightfall, which in those latitudes arrives when it is still only mid-afternoon in Spain, we headed south-west, leaving behind us a scene of fires, shipwrecks and desolation.

There were no further incidents apart from the discomforts of the voyage itself, if we discount the three days of storms halfway between Ireland and

Cape Finisterre, which flung us about below decks and had us all saying our paternosters and our Ave Marias – indeed, before it could be secured, a loose cannon in the *San Lorenzo* rammed several men against a bulkhead, crushing them like bedbugs – leaving the galleon so much the worse for wear that in the end she limped off to seek shelter at Vigo. Then came the alarming news that the English were once again attacking Cádiz, something we learned only in Lisbon. And so, while some escort ships detailed for the Indies route headed off for the Azores in order to warn the treasure fleet and provide it with reinforcements, we set sail for Cádiz, just in time, as I said, to see the backs of the English.

I made use of the voyage to read, with great delight and profit, Mateo Alemán's *Guzmán de Alfarache*, and other books that Captain Alatriste had either brought with him or acquired on board; these were, if I remember rightly, *The Life of the Squire, Marcos de Obregón*, a volume of Suetonius and the second part of *The Ingenious Gentleman Don Quijote de la Mancha*. There was also, as far as I was concerned, a practical aspect to the voyage which would in time prove extremely useful, for after my experiences in Flanders, where I had acquired all the skills of war, Captain Alatriste and his colleagues took it upon themselves to train me in swordplay. I was rapidly approaching the age of sixteen; my body had filled out; and the hardships endured in Flanders had strengthened my

11

limbs, tested my mettle and toughened my resolve. Diego Alatriste knew better than anyone that a steel blade can place the most humble man on the same footing as a monarch, and that when all the cards are stacked against you, knowing how to handle a fine piece of Toledo steel provides a more than decent way of earning one's daily bread – or indeed of defending it. To complete my education, begun in the harsh school of Flanders, he decided to teach me the secrets of fencing, and to this end every day we would seek out a part of the deck where our comrades would make room for us or even form a circle to watch with expert eyes, proffering opinions and advice and larding these comments with accounts of feats and exploits sometimes more imagined than real. In this world of connoisseurs and experts – for, as I once said, there is no better fencing master than the man who has felt cold steel in his own flesh – Captain Alatriste and I practised thrusts, feints, attacks and retreats, strikes performed with the palm up and with the palm down, wounds inflicted with the point of the sword and with the edge of the blade itself, and various other techniques at the disposal of the professional swordsman. Thus I learned all the tricks of the trade: how to grab my opponent's sword and then drive my blade into his chest; how to draw my blade back, slashing his face as I did so; how to slice and to thrust with both sword and dagger; how to use a lantern to dazzle, or even the light of the sun; how to make unashamed use of feet and elbows; and the many ways of wrapping my cloak around my opponent's blade and then finishing him off in a trice. In short, I learned everything that goes to make a skilled swordsman. And although we could not know it at the time, I would soon be presented with an opportunity to put all of this into practice, for a letter awaited us in Cádiz, along with a friend in Seville and an extraordinary adventure that would take place at the mouth of the Guadalquivir river. But all of this I will unfold in the fullness of time.

Dear Captain Alatriste

You will perhaps be surprised to receive this letter, which serves, first and foremost, to welcome you on your return to Spain, a voyage which I hope has been happily concluded.

Thanks to the news you sent me from Antwerp – where your face, bold Spaniard, doubtless made even the River Scheldt grow pale – I have been able to follow your steps, and I hope that, despite cruel Neptune's traps, you continue safe and well, as does, too, our dear Íñigo. If so, you will have arrived at precisely the right moment. For if, upon your advent in Cádiz, the Indies fleet has still not arrived, I must ask you to come at once to Seville by whatever means possible. The King is currently in this city of Betis, on a visit to Andalusia with Her Majesty the Queen, and since I am thankfully still in favour with Philip IV and with his Atlas, the Count-Duke of Olivares (although of course yesterday is gone, tomorrow has not yet come, and one untimely sonnet or epigram could easily cost me another period of exile in my personal Ponto Euxino, Torre de Juan Abad), I am here in his illustrious company, doing a little of everything and apparently a great deal of nothing, at least officially. As to the unofficial, I will tell you about that in detail when I have the pleasure of once more embracing you in Seville. I can say no more until then, only to remark that since the matter requires your participation, it is (naturally) a matter requiring swords.

I send you my very warmest regards, and greetings also from the Count of Guadalmedina, who is here with me, looking as handsome as ever and busily seducing all the ladies of Seville.

Your friend, always,
Francisco de Quevedo Villegas

Diego Alatriste put the letter away in his doublet and climbed into the skiff beside me amongst the bundles containing our luggage. The boatmen's voices rang out as they leaned upon the oars that splashed in the water, and we gradually left behind us the *Jesús Nazareno*, where it lay motionless in the still water along with the other galleons, so imposing with their high, pitch-black sides, their red paint and gilt glinting in the daylight, the spars

14

and tangled rigging rising into the sky. Shortly afterwards we were back on land, feeling the ground sway beneath our uncertain feet. After weeks confined to the deck of a ship, it was bewildering to be amongst so many people and with so much space in which to move about. We delighted in the food on display outside the shops: oranges, lemons, raisins, plums, salt meat and fish, the white bread in the bakeries, the pungent smell of spices, and the familiar voices touting all kinds of unusual goods and merchandise: paper from Genoa, wax from Barbary, wines from Sanlúcar, Jerez and El Puerto, sugar from Motril . . . The captain stopped at a barber's, who shaved him and trimmed his hair and moustache, and I remained at his side, gazing happily about me. In those days Cádiz had not yet displaced Seville in importance as regards the route to and from the Indies, and the city was still small with only four or five inns and taverns, but its streets, frequented by people from Genoa and Portugal, and by black slaves and Moors, were bathed in a dazzling light, the air was transparent, and everything was bright and cheerful – a world away from Flanders. There was barely a trace of the recent battle, although everywhere one saw soldiers and armed civilians, and the cathedral square, our next stop after the barber's, was packed with people bound for church to give thanks to God that the city had been saved from being plundered and burned. As arranged, a messenger, a freed black slave sent by

15

Don Francisco de Quevedo, was waiting for us there, and while we took a cool drink at an inn and ate a few slices of tuna with white bread and green beans drizzled with olive oil, he explained the situation. After the alarm provoked by the English attack, every horse in town had been requisitioned, and the surest way therefore to reach Seville was to cross over to El Puerto de Santa María, where the King's galleys were anchored, and there board a galley that was preparing to sail up the Guadalquivir to Seville. The messenger had, he said, arranged for a small boat with a skipper and four sailors to take us to El Puerto, and so we returned to the port and on the way were given documents signed by the Duke of Fernandina, a passport granting free passage and embarkation as far as Seville 'to Diego Alatriste y Tenorio, one of the King's soldiers on leave from Flanders, and to his servant Íñigo Balboa Aguirre'.

In the port, where bundles of soldiers' luggage and equipment were being piled high, we bade farewell to the few comrades still lingering there – as caught up in their card games as they were with the local whores, who, in their distinctive half-capes, were taking full advantage of the recent disembarkation to seize what booty they could. When we said our goodbyes, Curro Garrote was already back on dry land, crouched beside a gaming table that guaranteed more tricks and surprises than spring itself, and playing cards as if his life depended on it, his doublet open and his one good hand resting, just in case, on the pommel of his dagger. His other hand travelled back and forth between his mug of wine and his cards, accompanied by curses, oaths and blasphemies, as he saw half the contents of his purse disappearing into someone else's. The *malagueño* nevertheless interrupted his activities to wish us luck, adding that he would see us again somewhere, here or there.

'And if not there,' he concluded, 'then in Hell.'

Next, we said goodbye to Sebastián Copons, who, as you will remember, was an old soldier from Huesca, small, thin and wiry, and even less given to talking than Captain Alatriste. Copons said that he was thinking of spending a few days leave in Cádiz and would then, like us, travel up to Seville. He was fifty, with many campaigns behind him and far too many scars on his body – the latest, earned at the Ruyter mill, had traced a line from his forehead to his ear – and it was, he said, perhaps time to be thinking about going back to Cillas de Ansó, the little village where he'd been born. A young wife and some land of his own would suit him fine – if, that is, he could get used to driving a spade into the earth rather than a sword into the guts of Lutherans. My master and he arranged to meet up again in Seville at Becerra's. And when they said goodbye, I noticed that they embraced in silence, with no fuss but with a stoicism typical of both.

I was sorry to leave Copons and Garrote, even though, despite all we'd been through together, I had never warmed to the latter, with his curly hair, his gold earring and his disreputable air, but they were the only two comrades from our company in Breda who had travelled back to Cádiz with us. All the others had, in one way or another, been left behind: Llop from Mallorca and Rivas from Galicia were lying six feet under the Flemish earth, one at the Ruyter mill and the other in the barracks at Terheyden. Mendieta from Vizcaya – assuming he was still alive to tell the tale – would be lying in a gloomy military hospital in Brussels, prostrated by the black vomit, while the Olivares brothers, taking with them as page my friend Jaime Correas, had re-enlisted for a new campaign in the regiment led by Don Francisco de Medina after our Cartagena regiment, which had suffered so much during the long siege of Breda, was temporarily disbanded. The war in Flanders had been going on for a long time, and it was said that, in view of all the money and lives the last few years had cost, the Count-Duke of Olivares, minister and favourite of our King Philip IV, had decided to place our army there on a defensive footing in order to cut expenses, reducing the fighting force to an indispensable minimum. The fact is that six thousand soldiers had been discharged, either voluntarily or by force, which is why the *Jesús Nazareno* was returning to Spain full of veterans, some of them old and infirm,

18

others having been paid off, either because they'd completed the regulation period of service or because they were being posted on to different regiments and units in Spain itself or around the Mediterranean. Many of them were weary of war and its perils, and might well have agreed with that character in a Lope de Vega play:

> *What have the Lutherans*
> *ever done to me?*
> *The Lord Jesus made them,*
> *and He can slay them –*
> *if He so chooses –*
> *far more easily than we.*

The freed slave sent by Don Francisco de Quevedo also took leave of us in Cádiz, having first shown us to our boat. We climbed aboard and were rowed away from the shore, and after we had again passed our imposing galleons – it was strange to see them from so low down – the skipper, judging that the wind was right, gave orders for the sail to be raised. Thus we crossed the bay, heading for the mouth of the Guadalete, and by evening we had joined the *Levantina*, an elegant galley anchored along with many others in the middle of the river – all with their lateen yards and spars tied up on deck – opposite the great salt mountains that rose like heaps of snow on the left bank. The city, white and tawny, stretched away to the right, with the tall castle tower protecting the mouth of the anchorage. El Puerto de Santa María was the main base for the King's galleys, and my master knew it from the time when he had set sail against the Turks and the Berbers. As for the galleys, those war machines propelled by human blood and muscle, he knew far more about them than most would care to. That is why, after presenting ourselves to the captain of the *Levantina*, who glanced at our passport and gave us permission to stay on board, Alatriste found us a comfortable place near a crossbow embrasure – having first greased the palm of the galley master in charge of the rabble with a silver piece of eight – and remained awake all night, his back resting against our luggage and his dagger at the ready. As he explained in a whisper, a faint smile on his lips, it would take at least three hundred years in Purgatory before even the most honest of galley slaves, from the captain down to the last forced man, was given his discharge papers and allowed into Heaven.

I slept wrapped in my blanket, untroubled by the cockroaches and lice scampering over me, for they were hardly a novelty after my experiences on our long voyage on the *Jesús Nazareno*. Any ship or vessel is home to gallant legions of rats, bedbugs, fleas and all manner of creeping things who are quite capable of eating a cabin boy alive and who observe neither Fridays nor Lent. And whenever

I woke to scratch myself, I would see close by me Diego Alatriste's wide eyes, as pale as if they were made of the same light as the moon that moved slowly above our heads and above the masts. I thought of his joke about galley slaves being discharged from Purgatory. The truth is I'd never heard him give a reason why he had asked Captain Bragado for us to be discharged after the Breda campaign, and I hadn't been able to get a word out of him either then or afterwards; however, I sensed that I might have had something to do with the decision. Only years later did I learn that at one point Alatriste had considered the possibility, amongst many others, of travelling with me to the Indies. As I have told you before, the captain had, in his fashion, looked after me ever since my father's death in battle at Jülich in the year 1621, and had apparently now reached the conclusion that after my experience with the army in Flanders – useful for a lad born into that particular period and with my particular talents, as long as I did not leave behind me my health, life and conscience – it was time to see to my education and prepare for my future by returning to Spain. Alatriste did not believe that a career as a soldier was the best choice for the son of his friend Lope Balboa, although I proved him wrong about that when, after Nördlingen, the defence of Fuenterrabía and the wars of Portugal and Catalonia, I was made ensign at Rocroi and, after leading a company of two hundred men, was appointed lieutenant of the

21

Royal Mail and later captain of the Spanish guard of King Philip IV. However, such a record only shows how right Diego Alatriste was, for although I fought honourably on many a battlefield like the good Catholic, Spaniard and Basque that I am, I gained but little reward, and what advantages and promotions I was given were due less to the military life itself and more to the favour of the King, to my relationship with Angélica de Alquézar and to the good fortune that has always accompanied me. For Spain, rarely a mother and more often a wicked stepmother, always pays very little for the blood of those who spill it in her service, and others with more merit than I were left to rot in the anterooms of indifferent functionaries, in homes for the old and frail or in convents, just as they had been abandoned to their fate in many a battle and left to fester in the trenches. I was the exception in enjoying good fortune, for in Alatriste's and my profession the normal end to a life spent watching bullets rain down on armour was this:

> *Broken, scarred and crippled,*
> *Carrying, if you're lucky, a letter,*
> *To present at the door of hospitals*
> *Where no one ever gets better.*

Not even asking for a reward, a benefice, the captaincy of a company or even bread for your children, but merely a little charity for having lost your arm in Lepanto, in Flanders or in Hell itself,

22

and instead seeing the door slammed shut in your face with the words:

> *So you served His Majesty*
> *And lost your arm?*
> *Bad luck, we say!*
> *But why, pray, should we pay*
> *For Flanders' harm?*

And then of course Captain Alatriste was growing older. Not old in years, you understand, for at the time – the end of the first quarter of the century – he must have been only a little over forty. I mean that he had grown old inside, as was the case with other men like him who had been fighting for the true religion ever since they were boys, receiving nothing in exchange but scars, travails and misfortunes. The Breda campaign, in which Alatriste had placed some hope for himself and for me, had proved hard and unrewarding, with unfair officers, cruel commanders, much sacrifice and little benefit. We were all as poor as we had been when we started two years before, apart, that is, from what we had managed to ransack from Oudkerk and from other pillaging expeditions, and not counting the discharge pay – my master's, for we servants were unpaid – which, in the form of a few silver escudos, would at least allow us to survive for a few months. Despite all this, the captain would go on to fight again, when life obliged us to serve once more under the Spanish flag, until I saw him die as I had seen him live: standing, his hair and moustache now grizzled, sword in hand, his eyes calm and indifferent, at the Battle of Rocroi, on the day when the best infantry in the world allowed themselves to be defeated merely in order to remain faithful to their King and to their own legend and glory. And thus, exactly as I had always known him, in good times, of which there were few, and in bad, of which there were many, Captain Alatriste died true to himself and to his own silences. Like a soldier.

But let us not anticipate stories or events. Long before that, as I was saying, something was already dying inside the man who was then my master. Something indefinable but of which I first became truly aware on the voyage that brought us back from Flanders. For all my youthful lucidity, however, I still did not quite understand what that something was, and could only watch as a part of Diego Alatriste slowly withered and died. Later, I decided it was a kind of faith, or the remnants of a faith, perhaps a faith in the human condition or in what heretical unbelievers call Fate and what decent men call God. Or perhaps it was the painful certainty that our poor Spain, and Alatriste with her, was sliding down into a bottomless pit with no hope of anyone getting her or us out of it, not for a long time, not for centuries. And I still wonder if my presence at his side, my youth and the adoring way I looked at him – for I worshipped

24

him then – did not force him to maintain his composure, a composure which in other circumstances might have drowned like mosquitoes in the wine, of which he occasionally drank far too much, or might else have found resolution in the black, definitive barrel of his pistol.

CHAPTER 2

A MATTER REQUIRING SWORDS

'There'll be some killing involved,' warned Don Francisco de Quevedo. 'Possibly a lot.'

'I only have two hands,' responded Alatriste.

'Four,' I said.

The captain kept his eyes trained on the mug of wine before him. Don Francisco adjusted his spectacles on his nose and studied my face for a moment before turning towards a man seated at a table at the far end of the room in a discreet corner of the inn. He had been there when we arrived, and our friend the poet had referred to him as Master Olmedilla with no further introduction or explanation, except that later he added the word 'accountant': the accountant Olmedilla. He was a small thin man, bald and very pale. He appeared timid and mouse-like, despite his black clothes and the little curled moustache that set off a short sparse beard. He had ink-stained fingers and the look of a pettifogging lawyer or government official who lives by candlelight, surrounded by files and papers. He gave a prudent nod to the silent question Don Francisco was asking him.

'There are two parts to the task,' Quevedo told the captain. 'The first will involve you helping that gentleman over there carry out certain, shall we say, negotiations,' and he indicated the little man, who remained entirely impassive under our scrutiny. 'For the second part, you can recruit as many men as you think necessary.'

'They'll require some payment in advance.'

'God will provide.'

'Since when have you involved God in these matters, Don Francisco?'

'You're right, but with or without him there will be no shortage of gold.'

He lowered his voice, whether at the mention of God or gold, I'm not sure. The two long years that had passed since our encounter with the Inquisition – when Don Francisco de Quevedo had plucked me from an auto-da-fé by dint of some very fast riding – had placed two more furrows on his forehead. He seemed somewhat weary as he toyed with his inevitable mug of wine, on this occasion a good white from Fuente del Maestre. The sunshine coming in through the window simultaneously caught the golden pommel of his sword and my hand resting on the table, and traced a line of light around Captain Alatriste's profile. Enrique Becerra's inn, famous for its lamb in honey sauce and stewed pork jowls, was near the public bawdy house in Compás de la Laguna, next to the Puerta del Arenal, and from the top floor, beyond the walls and the flat roof where the whores hung their linen out to dry, could be seen the masts and pennants of ships moored in Triana, on the far side of the river.

'As you see, Captain,' added the poet, 'once again, there's nothing for it but to fight . . . although, this time I will not be coming with you.'

Now he was smiling in a friendly reassuring fashion with that singular affection he always reserved for us.

'Well,' muttered Alatriste, 'we each have our own fate to follow.'

He was dressed entirely in brown, with a suede doublet, a flat Walloon collar, canvas breeches and military-style gaiters. He had left his last pair of boots, their soles full of holes, on board the *Levantina*, having swapped them with the sub-galley master for some dried mullet roes, boiled beans and a wineskin to sustain us on the journey upriver. For this and other reasons, my master did not seem particularly upset to find that the first thing he should meet with when setting foot again on Spanish soil was an invitation to return to his old profession. Perhaps because the commission came from a friend or perhaps because, according to that friend, the commission came from much higher up, but mainly, I suspect, because the purse we had brought back with us from Flanders made not a sound when shaken. From time to time the captain would regard me thoughtfully, as if wondering just where my nearly sixteen years and the skills he had taught me fitted in with all this.

I didn't wear a sword of course and only a misericord – a dagger of mercy – hung from my belt at my back, but I had been tried and tested in the fire of war; I was bright, quick and brave and very useful when called upon to serve. The question Alatriste was asking himself, I suppose, was whether to include or exclude me. Although, given the way things were, he could no longer make that decision alone; for good or ill, our lives were intertwined. And as he had just remarked, each man has to follow his own fate. As for Don Francisco, to judge by the way he was looking at me, astonished at how I'd shot up and at the fuzz of hair on my upper lip and cheeks, I guessed that he was thinking exactly the same: I had reached the age when a lad is just as capable of dealing out sword thrusts as receiving them.

'And Íñigo goes too,' he said.

I knew my master well enough to know when to keep silent, which is precisely what I did, following his example and staring into the mug of wine on the table before me – for as regards wine too I had grown up. Don Francisco's comment was not a question, merely affirmation of an obvious fact, and after a silence Alatriste nodded slowly and resignedly. He did so without even looking at me, and I felt an inner surge of joy, bright and strong, which I concealed by taking a sip of wine. It tasted to me of glory, maturity, adventure.

'So let's drink to Íñigo,' said Quevedo.

We drank, and the accountant Olmedilla, that small pale fellow all in black, joined us not by raising his glass but with another brief nod of his head. As for the captain, Don Francisco and myself, this was not our first toast of the day since the three of us had embraced at the pontoon bridge connecting Triana and El Arenal after we had disembarked from the *Levantina*. The captain and I had sailed along the coast from El Puerto de Santa María, past Rota, before crossing the bar at Sanlúcar and continuing on to Seville, passing first the great pine woods growing along the sandy banks and then, further upriver, the dense groves of trees, orchards and forests on the shores of what the Arabs called Wadi el Kebir, the Great River. In contrast, what I remember most about that journey is the stink of dirt and sweat, the galley master's whistle marking time, the laboured breathing of the galley slaves and the clink of their chains as the oars entered and left the water with rhythmic precision, driving the galley forward against the current. The galley master, sub-galley master and constable walked up and down the gangway, keeping a watchful eye on their parishioners, and every now and then the whip would come down hard on the bare back of some idler and weave him a doublet of lashes. It was painful to watch the oarsmen, one hundred and twenty men seated on twenty-four benches, five to each oar, with their shaven heads and heavily bearded faces, their torsos shining with sweat as they rose and fell, working the long oars. There were Moorish slaves, former Turkish pirates and renegades, as well as Christians serving sentences meted out by a justice which they had not gold enough to buy. Alatriste said to me: 'Never let them get you onto one of these ships alive.'

His cold, pale, inscrutable eyes were watching the poor unfortunates row. As I said, my master knew this world well, for he had served as a soldier on the galleys of the Naples regiment during the Battle of La Goleta and in attacks on the Kerkennah Islands; and after fighting Venetians and Berbers he himself, in 1613, had come very close to being forced to serve on a Turkish galley. Later, when I was one of the King's soldiers, I too sailed the Mediterranean on these ships, and I can assure you that few seaborne inventions bear a closer resemblance to Hell. To give a measure of the harshness of a galley slave's life, suffice it to say that even for the very worst crimes the term meted out was never more than ten years on the galleys, for this was calculated to be the maximum length of time any man could survive without losing his health, reason and life to hardship and the lash.

> *Take off the man's shirt,*
> *To wash his soft flesh,*
> *See what's written by the lash,*
> *Bold and bloody 'neath the dirt.*

31

Thus, by dint of whistle and oar, we had travelled up the Guadalquivir and arrived in the most fascinating city, trading port and marketplace in the world, a gold and silver galleon anchored between glory and misery, opulence and profligacy in the capital of the Ocean Sea and of all the wealth brought by the annual treasure fleet from the Indies; a city populated by nobles, merchants, clerics, rogues and alluring women; a city so rich, powerful and beautiful that neither Tyre nor Alexandria in their day could have equalled it. Homeland and home to all who came to her, a place of inexhaustible marvels, a mother to orphans and a cloak for sinners, just like the Spain of those wretched and magnificent times, a place where poverty was everywhere, and yet where no one capable of scraping a living need ever be poor. Where everything was wealth, but where – like life itself – it took but a moment's inattention to lose it all.

We spent a long time at the inn talking but without exchanging one word with the accountant Olmedilla; however, as soon as he stood up to leave, Quevedo instructed us to go after him, following at a distance. It would be a good thing, he explained, for Captain Alatriste to familiarise himself with the man. We walked along Calle de Tintores, astonished at the number of foreigners frequenting the inns there, then we set off for Plaza de San Francisco and the cathedral, and from there, via Calle del Aceite, we reached the mint, near the Torre del Oro, where Olmedilla had some business to attend to. As you can imagine, I, wide-eyed, was busily taking everything in: the newly swept doorways where women were emptying out their wash bowls or planting up pots with flowers; the shops selling soap, spices, jewels and swords; the boxes of produce outside the fruitshops; the gleaming basins that hung above the door of every barber; the street traders; the ladies accompanied by their duennas; the men haggling; the grave-faced canons mounted on their mules; the black and Moorish slaves; the houses painted in red ochre and white-wash; the churches with their glazed tile roofs; the palaces; the orange and lemon trees; the crosses placed at the corners of streets to commemorate some violent death or simply to discourage passers-by from relieving them-selves . . . And even though it was still winter, everything glittered beneath a splendid sun that caused my master and Don Francisco to fold up their cloaks and wear them slung crosswise over chest and shoulder and to throw back their capes and undo the loops and buttons on their doublets. The knowledge that the King and Queen were both in Seville only added to the natural beauty of the place, and that celebrated city and its more than one hundred thousand inhabitants bubbled with excitement and jubilation. Unusually, that year King Philip IV was preparing to honour with his august presence the arrival of the treasure fleet,

33

which would be bringing with it a fortune in gold and silver to be distributed, unfortunately for us, to the rest of Europe and the world. The overseas empire that had been created a century before by Cortés, Pizarro and other adventurers with few scruples and a great deal of pluck, with nothing to lose but their lives and with everything to gain, now provided a constant flow of wealth that allowed Spain to pay for the wars in which it was embroiled with half the known world, wars waged in defence of our military hegemony and of the one true religion. That money was all the more necessary, were that possible, in a country where – as I have said – absolutely everyone gave himself airs, work was frowned upon, commerce held in low esteem and the dream of every scoundrel was to be granted letters patent of nobility and thus live a life free from taxes and travail. Young men understandably preferred to try their fortune in the Indies or in Flanders rather than languish in Spain's barren fields, at the mercy of an idle clergy, an ignorant decadent aristocracy and a corrupt bureaucracy eager to suck the blood and life out of them. It is said – and it is very true – that the moment vice becomes custom marks the death of a republic, for the dissolute person ceases to be considered loathsome, and all baseness is seen as normal. It was thanks to the rich deposits in the Americas that Spain was able, for so long, to maintain an empire based on that abundance of gold and silver and on the quality of its coinage, which served both to pay the armies – when indeed they were paid – and to import foreign goods and products; for although we could send flour, oil, vinegar and wine to the Indies, everything else came from abroad. This obliged us to go elsewhere for supplies, and our much-valued gold doubloons and famous silver pieces of eight played a major role. We survived thanks to the vast quantities of coins and bars of gold that travelled from Mexico and Peru to Seville, whence they were immediately scattered throughout the other countries of Europe and even the Orient, ending up as far away as India and China. The truth is that all this wealth benefited everyone except the Spanish: since the Crown was always in debt, the money was spent before it had even arrived; and as soon as it was disembarked, the gold left Spain to be squandered in those lands where we were at war, vanishing into the Genoese and Portuguese banks who were our creditors and even into the hands of our enemies. To quote Don Francisco de Quevedo:

In the Indies he was born an honest man,
When all the world admired his purity,
But in Spain he spent both substance and security
And, losing life and interest, died a Genoan.
But anyone who claims to be his kinsman,
Howe'er sour-faced, becomes as sweet as honey,
For he remains a powerful gentleman,
Does our Sir Money.

The umbilical cord that kept our poor – and paradoxically rich – Spain breathing was the treasure fleet, which sailed the seas as much at risk from hurricanes as from pirates. This was why its arrival in Seville provoked indescribable celebration, for as well as the gold and silver destined for the King and for certain individuals, it also brought with it cochineal, indigo, logwood, Brazil wood, wool, cotton, hides, sugar, tobacco and spices, not forgetting chilli, ginger and Chinese silk brought from the Philippines via Acapulco. To this end our galleons sailed in convoy from New Spain and Tierra Firme as far as Cuba, where they formed one gigantic fleet. And it has to be said that, during all this time, despite dearth, disaster and difficulty, the Spanish sailors carried out their work with great pride. Even at the very worst moments – when, for example, the Dutch captured an entire fleet – our ships continued to cross the sea through great effort and sacrifice, and except on certain unfortunate occasions always managed to keep at bay the threat from the French, Dutch and English pirates during a struggle in which Spain fought alone against those three powerful nations, all set on having a share of the spoils.

'Not many bluebottles about,' commented Alatriste laconically.

This was true. The fleet was about to arrive; the King was honouring Seville with his presence;

36

religious ceremonies and public celebrations were being organised, and yet there was hardly a catch-pole or constable to be seen in the streets. The few we passed were standing in groups, armed to the teeth, with more steel on them than a Basque foundry, fearful even of their own shadows.

'There was an incident four days ago,' Quevedo told us. 'The law officers tried to arrest a soldier on one of the galleys moored in Triana, but the other soldiers and conscripts went to his aid, and people were being knifed left, right and centre . . . In the end the catchpoles managed to drag the man off to jail, but the soldiers surrounded the place and threatened to set fire to it if they weren't given back their comrade.'

'And how did the matter end?'

'Since the prisoner had killed a constable, the officers hanged him from the railings before handing him back.' The poet chuckled as he described what had happened. 'So now the soldiers are on the hunt for constables, and the constables only dare go about in gangs and even then only with great caution.'

'And what does the King have to say about it all?'

We were standing in the shadow of the gateway known as the Postigo del Carbón, immediately below the Torre de la Plata, while the accountant Olmedilla sorted out his business at the mint. Quevedo pointed to the walls of the ancient Moorish castle that extended as far as the cathedral's

37

immensely tall belltower. The red and yellow uniforms of the Spanish guard stood out brightly against the battlements emblazoned with the King's coat of arms; little did we imagine that many years later I myself would wear that uniform. More sentinels bearing halberds and harquebuses kept watch at the main gate.

'His Sacred Catholic Royal Majesty knows what he's told, nothing more,' said Quevedo. 'The great Philip is staying at the Alcázar and only leaves there to go hunting or for a party or a night-time visit to some convent . . . Our friend Guadalmedina, by the way, is acting as escort. They have become close friends.'

The word 'convent' spoken in that tone of voice brought back grim memories, and I couldn't help but shudder when I remembered poor Elvira de la Cruz and how close I too had come to being burned at the stake. Don Francisco de Quevedo had meanwhile been distracted by the sight of a rather attractive lady. She was accompanied by her duenna and a Morisco slave girl laden with baskets and packages, and when she lifted the hem of her dress to avoid the trail of dung caking the street, she revealed fashionable corksoled clogs. As the lady passed us on her way to the muledrawn coach waiting a little further on, the poet adjusted the spectacles on his nose and very courteously doffed his hat. 'Lisi,' he murmured with a melancholy smile. The lady reciprocated with a slight nod before drawing her cloak more closely about her.

Behind her, the ageing duenna, clothed in deepest mourning, wearing a crow-black wimple and clutching a rosary, shot him a withering look. Quevedo stuck his tongue out at her. As he watched them depart, he smiled sadly and turned back to us without a word of explanation. He was dressed as soberly as ever: black silk stockings and shoes with silver buckles, a sombre grey costume, a hat of the same colour with a white feather, and the cross of St James embroidered in red beneath the short cape caught back on his shoulder.

'Convents are his speciality,' he added after that brief pensive pause, his eyes still fixed on the lady and her companions.

'Guadalmedina's or the King's?' Now it was Alatriste who was smiling beneath his soldierly moustache.

Quevedo took a while to respond, then, sighing deeply, he said, 'Both.'

I positioned myself next to the poet and, with eyes downcast, asked, 'And the Queen?'

I asked this in a casual, respectful, irreproachable tone, as if it were the mere curiosity of a boy. Don Francisco turned a penetrating eye on me.

'As lovely as ever,' he answered. 'She now speaks the language of Spain a little better than she did.' He glanced at Alatriste and then back at me, his eyes glinting merrily behind the lenses of his spectacles. 'She practises with her ladies-in-waiting and her mistress of the robes . . . and with her maids of honour.'

My heart was beating so fast I was afraid it might give me away.

'Did they all accompany her on the journey?'

'They did.'

The street was spinning. *She* was in this fascinating city. I gazed around me: at the empty sandy area known as El Arenal, one of the most picturesque parts of Seville, which stretched from the city walls down to the Guadalquivir, with Triana on the far shore; at the sails on the sardine boats and the shrimpers, and at all the other little boats coming and going; at the King's galleys moored over by Triana, which was crammed with vessels as far as the pontoon; at El Altozano and the sinister castle which was the seat of the Inquisition; at the crowd of great ships on the near shore: a forest of masts, spars, lateen yards, sails and flags; at the swarms of people, the tradesmen's stalls, the bundles of merchandise. I could hear the hammering of ship's carpenters, see the smoke from the caulkers' tar barrels and the pulleys on the great naval crane at the mouth of the Tagarete which was used to careen the ships' bottoms.

The Basques in the north send us wood,
And cloth and iron and ships true and good,
And the sailor brings from the brave New World
Ambergris, pearls, silver and gold,
And skins and strange exotic dyes,
And everything else that money buys.

Lope de Vega's play *El Arenal de Sevilla*, from which these lines come, had remained engraved on my memory ever since I first saw it with Captain Alatriste at the openair theatre of El Príncipe when I was a mere boy, on the famous day when Buckingham and the Prince of Wales had fought alongside him. And suddenly that place, that city which was in itself so splendid, was transformed into something magical and marvellous. Angélica de Alquézar was there, and I might perhaps see her. I gave a sideways glance at my master, fearful that my inner turbulence might be visible from without. Fortunately, Diego Alatriste had more worrying things on his mind. He was studying the accountant Olmedilla, who had finished his business and was walking towards us, eyeing us about as cordially as if we had come to administer the last rites. Grave-faced and dressed entirely in black apart from his white ruff, and wearing a narrow-brimmed black hat unadorned by any feather, and with that curious sparse beard which only accentuated his grey mouse-like appearance, he had the pinched air of one plagued by acid humours and bad digestion.

'What do we need with this fool?' muttered the captain as he watched him approach.

Quevedo shrugged. 'He's been given a mission to fulfil. The Count-Duke himself is pulling the strings. And Master Olmedilla's work will discomfit quite a number of people.'

Olmedilla greeted us with a curt nod, and we

followed him to the Triana gate. Alatriste spoke to Quevedo in a low voice: 'What exactly does he do?'

The poet responded equally softly, 'As I said, he's an accountant, an expert at balancing books . . . A man who knows everything there is to know about figures, customs duties and suchlike. Why, he could outshine the mathematician Juan de Leganés.'

'Has someone been stealing more than he should?'

'There is always someone stealing more than he should.'

The broad brim of Alatriste's hat cast a shadow over his face, a mask that only emphasised the paleness of his eyes, in which the light and the landscape of El Arenal were reflected.

'And where exactly do *we* fit in with all of this?'

'I'm only acting as intermediary. I am currently much in favour at Court. The King requires me to be witty, and the Queen laughs at my jokes. As for the Count-Duke, I do him the occasional small favour, and he repays me in kind.'

'I'm glad to see that Fortune is finally smiling on you.'

'Don't speak too loudly. Fortune has played so many tricks on me in the past, I view her very warily indeed.'

Alatriste observed the poet, amused. 'Nevertheless, Don Francisco, you certainly look every inch the courtier.'

'Oh please, Captain!' Quevedo was tugging at

his ruff where it irritated his skin. 'Being an artist and enjoying regular hot meals are two activities that are rarely compatible. I am simply having a run of good luck at the moment: I'm popular and my poetry is being read everywhere. As usual, I even have attributed to me poems I did not write, including some monstrosities by that bugger, that Babylonian, that sodomite Góngora, whose grandparents spurned bacon and worked as cobblers in Córdoba and whose "letters patent" you'll find hanging from the cathedral ceiling, along with the names of other Jews. Indeed, I have just hailed his latest published work with a delicate little poem of my own, which ends thus:

> *Be not flatulent,*
> *Vilest of sewers,*
> *Through which Parnassus*
> *Purges its excrement!*

'But to return to more serious matters. As I was saying, it's convenient for the Count-Duke to have me on his side. He flatters me and uses me. As for your involvement in the matter, Captain, that is a mere caprice on the part of the Count-Duke himself. For some reason he remembers you. Given we're talking about Olivares, that of course could be a good or a bad thing. Perhaps, in this instance, it's good. Besides, you did once offer him the services of your sword if he would help save Íñigo.'

Alatriste darted a glance at me, and then nodded slowly and pensively.

'He has a damnably good memory, the Count-Duke,' he said.

'Yes, when it suits him.'

My master again turned his attention to the accountant Olmedilla, who was walking a few paces ahead through the hustle and bustle of the harbour, his hands behind his back and a sour look on his face.

'He's not much of a talker,' Alatriste commented.

'No,' said Quevedo, laughing. 'In that respect, you and he should get along famously.'

'Is he a man of consequence?'

'As I said, he is merely an official, but he was put in charge of collating all the evidence when Don Rodrigo Calderón was put on trial for embezzlement. Now are you convinced?'

He fell silent to allow the captain to absorb the implications of this statement. Alatriste whistled through his teeth. The public execution a few years ago of a powerful figure like Calderón had shaken all of Spain.

'And whose trail is he on now?'

The poet declined to answer at first and for a while said nothing. Then, at last, he spoke: 'Someone will tell you all about that tonight. As for Olmedilla's mission, and indirectly yours, shall we just say that the commission comes from the Count-Duke, but the impulse behind it comes from the King himself.'

Alatriste shook his head incredulously. 'You are joking, aren't you, Don Francisco?'

'On my faith, I am not. Devil take me if I am, or may that humpbacked little playwright Ruiz de Alarcón suck all the talent from my brain.'

'God's blood!'

'That's exactly what I said when they asked me to be a third party in the matter. On the positive side, if things turn out well, you'll have a few escudos to spend.'

'And if things turn out badly?'

'Then I'm afraid you'll wish you were back in the trenches at Breda.' Quevedo sighed and looked around him like someone hoping to change the subject. 'I'm just sorry that for the moment I can tell you no more.'

'I don't need to know much more,' said my master, a mixture of irony and resignation dancing in his grey-green eyes. 'I just want to know from which side to expect an attack.'

Quevedo shrugged.

'From every side, as usual,' he replied, still gazing indifferently about him. 'You're not in Flanders now, Captain Alatriste. This is Spain.'

They arranged to meet again that night at Becerra's. The accountant Olmedilla, still looking glummer than a butcher's shop in Lent, withdrew to an inn in Calle de Tintores where he had his lodgings and where there was also a room reserved for us. My master spent the afternoon sorting out his affairs, getting his military licence certified and buying new linen and supplies – as well as a new pair of boots – with the money Don Francisco had advanced him for the work ahead. As for me, I was free for a few hours and went for a stroll into the heart of the city, enjoying the walks around the walls and the atmosphere in the streets with their low arches, coats of arms, crosses and retables depicting Christs, Virgins and saints – streets far too narrow for the carriages and horses that jammed them; a place at once dirty and opulent, seething with life: with knots of people at the doors of taverns and tenements, and women – whom I eyed with new interest since my experiences in Flanders – dark-skinned, neat and self-assured, who spoke with an accent that lent a special sweetness to their conversation. I saw mansions with magnificent courtyard gardens glimpsed through wrought-iron gates, with chains on the door to show they were immune from ordinary justice, and I sensed that while the Castilian nobility, in their determination not to work, took their stoicism to the point of ruin, the Seville aristocracy had a more relaxed approach and often allowed the words 'hidalgo' and 'merchant' to be conjoined. Thus the aristocrat did not scorn commerce if it brought him money, and the merchant was prepared to spend a fortune in order to be considered a hidalgo – even tailors required purity of blood from the members of their guild. This gave rise, on the one hand, to the spectacle of debased noblemen using their influence and privileges to prosper by underhand means, and, on the other, it meant that the work and commerce so vital to the nation continued to be frowned upon and consequently fell into the hands of foreigners. Thus, most of the Seville nobility were rich plebeians who had bought their way into a higher stratum of society through money and advantageous marriages, and now felt ashamed of their former trades. A generation of merchants spawned in turn a generation of 'noble', entirely parasitic heirs, who denied the origins of their fortune and squandered it without a qualm, thus proving the truth of that old Spanish saying: 'From tradesman to gentleman to gambler to beggar in four generations.'

I also visited the Alcaicería, the old silk market, an area full of shops selling rich merchandise and jewels. I was wearing black breeches and soldier's gaiters, a leather belt with my dagger stuck in at the back, a military-style jerkin over my much-darned shirt, and on my head a very elegant cap of Flemish velvet – the spoils of war from what were fast becoming the 'old days'. That and my youth both favoured me, I think, and adopting the air of a battle-hardened veteran I idled along past the swordsmiths' shops in Calle de la Mar and Calle de Vizcaínos, or past the braggarts, doxies and pimps in Calle de las Sierpes, opposite the famous prison behind whose black walls Mateo Alemán had languished and where good Don Miguel de

Cervantes had also spent some time. I swaggered past the legendary steps of the cathedral – that cathedral of villainy – which teemed with sellers, idlers and beggars with signs hanging round their necks and displaying wounds and deformities, each one falser than a Judas kiss, as well as people who had been crippled on the rack but claimed to have been wounded in Flanders. Some sported real or fake amputations which they attributed to days spent fighting at Antwerp or Mamora but which could as easily have been acquired at Roncevaux or at Numantia, for one had only to look them in the face, these men – who claimed to have won their scars for the sake of the true religion, King and country – to know that the closest they had come to a heretic or a Turk was in the safety of the audience at the local playhouse.

I ended up outside the Reales Alcázares, staring up at the Habsburg flag that flew above the battlements and at the imposing soldiers of the King's guard armed with halberds, standing to attention at the great gate. I wandered around there for a while, amongst the citizens eager to catch a glimpse of the King or Queen, should they chance to enter or leave. And when the crowd, and I amongst them, happened to move too close to the entrance, a sergeant in the Spanish guard came over to tell us rudely to leave. The other onlookers obeyed at once, but I, being my father's son, was piqued by the soldier's bad manners, and so I dawdled there with a haughty look on my face that clearly nettled him. He gave me a shove, and I – for my youth and my recent experience in Flanders had made me prickly about such matters – thought this the act of a scoundrel, so I rounded on him like a fierce young hound, my hand on the hilt of my dagger. The sergeant, a burly moustachioed type, roared with laughter.

'Oh, so you fancy yourself a swashbuckler, do you?' he said, looking me up and down. 'Aren't you a little too young for that, boy?'

I brazenly held his gaze, with the scorn of a veteran, which despite my youth I was. This fat fool had spent the last two years eating hot food, strolling about royal palaces and fortresses in his red and yellow chequered uniform, while I had been fighting alongside Captain Alatriste and watching my comrades die in Oudkerk, at the Ruyter mill, in Terheyden and in the prison cells of Breda, or else foraging for food in enemy territory with the Dutch cavalry at my back. How very unfair it was, I thought, that human beings did not carry their service record written on their face. Then I remembered Captain Alatriste, and I said to myself, by way of consolation, that some people did. Perhaps one day, I thought, people would know or guess what I had done simply by looking at me, and then all these sergeants, fat or thin, whose lives had never depended on their sword, would have to swallow their sarcasm.

'I may be young, but my dagger isn't,' I said resolutely.

The other man blinked; he had not expected such a riposte. I saw that he was taking a closer look at me. This time he noticed that I had my hand behind me, resting on the damascened hilt of my knife. Then he gazed dumbly into my eyes, incapable of reading what was in them.

'A pox on't, why I'll . . .'

The sergeant was fuming, and it certainly wasn't incense that was issuing forth from him. He raised his hand to slap me, which is the most unacceptable of offences – in the olden days one could only slap a man who wasn't dressed in the knightly uniform of helmet and coat of mail – and I said to myself, *I'm done for. Avenging every little slight can all too swiftly lead to death. Here I am in a situation from which there is no escape, and all because my name is Íñigo Balboa Aguirre and I'm from Oñate, and, more to the point, because I have just returned from Flanders and my master is Captain Alatriste, and I cannot consider as too costly any market where one buys one's honour with one's life. Whether I like it or not, every path is blocked, and so when I grasp my dagger I will have no option but to stab this fat pig in the belly – one thrust and it's done – and then run like a deer and get myself a hiding place, and just hope that nobody finds me.* In short – as Don Francisco de Quevedo would have said – there was, as usual, nothing for it but to fight. And so I held my breath and with the fatalistic resignation of the veteran – a recently acquired characteristic – prepared myself for what would follow. It seems, however, that God

50

spends his spare moments protecting arrogant young men, because just then a bugle sounded, the palace gates were flung wide open and there came the sound of wheels and hooves on gravel. The sergeant, mindful of his duty, immediately forgot all about me and ran to marshal his men; I stayed where I was, greatly relieved, thinking that I'd had a very lucky escape.

Carriages were leaving the palace, and when I noticed the insignia on the coach and saw the cavalry escort, I realised that it was our Queen, accompanied by her ladies-in-waiting and her mistress of the robes. My heart, which during the episode with the sergeant had remained steady and firm, suddenly bolted as if it had been given its head. Everything around me was spinning. The carriages rolled past to the sound of cheering and hallooing from the crowd, who rushed forward to greet it, and one pale royal hand, lovely and bejewelled, waved elegantly at one of the windows, in genteel response to this tribute from the people. I had other interests, however, and in each of the carriages that passed I eagerly sought the source of my unease. As I did so I took off my cap and drew myself up, standing hatless and motionless before the fleeting visions of lace, satin and furbelows, of female heads with coiffed and ringleted hair, of faces covered by fans, and of hands waving. In the last coach I glimpsed a fair head and a pair of blue eyes that saw me as they passed, recognising me with startled intensity before the vision moved off, and I was left there overwhelmed, watching the hunched back of the footman at the rear of the carriage and the dust covering the rumps of the guards' horses.

Then behind me I heard a whistle, one that I would have recognised in Hell itself. *Tirurí-ta-ta*. And when I turned, I found myself face to face with a ghost.

'You've grown, boy.'

Gualterio Malatesta was looking straight into my eyes, and I was sure that he could read my every thought. He was as ever dressed all in black, wearing a black hat with a very broad brim and, hanging from his leather baldric, the usual threatening sword with the long cross-guard. He was still very tall and thin, with that face of his devastated by pockmarks and scars, which gave him such a cadaverous tortured appearance that even the smile he directed at me, far from softening his features, only emphasised them.

'You've grown,' he said again. He seemed about to add 'since the last time' but did not. The 'last time' had been on the road to Toledo, when he had driven me in a closed carriage to the dungeons of the Inquisition. For very different reasons the memory of that adventure was as unpalatable to him as it was to me.

'And how is Captain Alatriste?'

I didn't answer; I merely held his gaze, which was as dark and fixed as that of a snake. When he spoke the name of my master the smile beneath his fine Italian-style moustache grew more dangerous.

'You remain a boy of few words, I see.'

He rested his left hand, gloved in black, on the guard of his sword and kept turning this way and that as if distracted. I heard him utter a soft sigh, almost of annoyance.

'So, in Seville too . . .' he said and then fell silent before I could fathom what he meant. After a while, with a glance and a lift of his chin, he indicated the sergeant of the Spanish guard, who was some way off, occupied with organising his men by the palace gate.

'I saw what happened between you. I was watching from the crowd.' He was studying me thoughtfully, as if assessing the changes that had taken place in me since the last time we had met. 'I see you are as punctilious as ever in matters of honour.'

'I've been in Flanders,' I blurted out. 'With the captain.'

He nodded. I noticed that there were a few grey hairs now in his moustache and in the side whiskers visible beneath the black brim of his hat, as well as a few new lines or scars on his face. *The years pass for everyone*, I thought. *Even for hired swordsmen with no heart.*

'I know,' he said, 'but regardless of whether you've been in Flanders or not you would do well to remember this: honour is a very complicated thing to acquire, difficult to preserve and dangerous to sustain . . . Ask your friend Alatriste.'

I stood up to him with all the firmness I could muster.

'Ask him yourself, if you've got the nerve.'

My sarcasm elicited not a flicker of response from his impassive face.

'I know the answer already,' he replied, unmoved. 'I have other less rhetorical matters pending with him.' He was still looking pensively in the direction of the guards at the gate. Then he chuckled to himself, as if at a joke he preferred not to share with anyone else.

'Some fools never learn,' he said suddenly. 'Like that imbecile who raised his hand to you without a thought for what you might do with yours.' The hard black snake eyes fixed on me again. 'If it had been me, I would never even have given you the chance to take that dagger out.'

I turned to observe the sergeant. He was strutting about keeping an eye on his soldiers while they closed the palace gates. And it was true: he was completely unaware how close he had come to having a span of steel in his guts and how close I had come to being hanged for his sake.

'Remember that the next time,' said the Italian.

When I turned back Gualterio Malatesta was no longer there. He had disappeared into the crowd, and all I could see was a black hat moving off past the orange trees beneath the cathedral belltower.

CHAPTER 3

CONSTABLES AND CATCHPOLES

That night would prove to be a long and busy one, but first there was time for supper and some interesting talk. There was also the unexpected arrival of a friend. Don Francisco de Quevedo had not told Captain Alatriste that the person he would be sharing supper with was none other than Álvaro de la Marca, Count of Guadalmedina. To Alatriste's surprise, and to mine, the Count appeared at Becerra's inn just after sunset, as cordial and self-assured as ever. He embraced the captain, patted me affectionately on the cheek and called loudly for good wine, a decent meal and a comfortable room in which he could converse with his companions.

'Now tell me all about Breda.'

Apart from the buff coat he was wearing, he was dressed very much in the style favoured by our King. His clothes were otherwise expensive but discreet, with no embroidery and no gold; he wore military boots, pale amber gloves, a hat and a long cloak; and tucked into his belt, as well as a sword and a dagger, was a pair of pistols. Don Álvaro's night would doubtless last long after his conversation with us, and towards dawn some husband or abbess would have good reason to keep one eye open as he or she slept. I remembered what Quevedo had said about the Count's role as companion to the King on the latter's nocturnal sorties.

'You look very well, Alatriste.'

'So do you, Count.'

'Oh, I take good care of myself, but make no mistake, my friend, at Court not working is very hard work indeed.'

He was still the same: handsome, elegant and with exquisite manners that were not in the least at odds with the easy, slightly rough, almost soldierly spontaneity with which he had always treated my master ever since the latter had saved his life during a disastrous Spanish attack on the Kerkennah Islands. He toasted Breda, Alatriste and even me; he argued with Don Francisco about the syllables in a sonnet, dispatched with an excellent appetite the lamb in honey sauce served up in good Triana earthenware, called for a clay pipe and tobacco and sat back in his chair wreathed in pipe smoke, with his buff coat unfastened and a contented look on his face.

'Now let's get down to serious matters,' he said.

Then, in between drawing on his pipe and taking sips of Aracena wine, he studied me for a moment as if calculating whether or not I should be listening to what he was about to say, and then he laid the facts before us. He began by explaining the system of fleets that transported the gold and silver. Seville's commercial monopoly and the strict controls imposed on who could and could not travel to the Indies had been devised to prevent foreign interference and smuggling, and to ensure the smooth running of the vast machinery of taxes, duties and tariffs on which the monarchy and its many parasites depended. That was the reason for the *almojarifazgo*, the customs cordon around Seville, Cádiz and its bay, which was the only port from which ships could embark for the Indies and disembark on their return. The royal coffers drew a large income from this, although it should be noted that, in a corrupt administration like Spain's, it was in the Crown's interest to let agents and other people in authority pay a fixed rate for their positions and then surreptitiously line their own pockets, stealing money hand over fist. In lean times, however, there was nothing to prevent the King occasionally imposing an exemplary fine or ordering the seizure of goods from private individuals who were travelling with the fleets.

'The problem,' said the Count, taking a couple of puffs on his pipe, 'is that all these taxes, which are intended to pay for the defence of our trade with the Indies, devour the very thing they're supposed to protect. A lot of gold and silver goes towards paying not only for the war in Flanders, but also for the widespread corruption and general apathy. And so merchants have to choose between two evils: being bled dry by the royal treasury or else indulging in a little contraband, all of which breeds a thriving criminal class.' He looked at Quevedo, smiling, soliciting his agreement. 'Isn't that so, Don Francisco?'

'Oh, yes,' agreed the poet. 'Here, even the fools are clever.'

'Or busy putting gold in their purses.'

'Very true.' Quevedo took a long drink of wine, then wiped his mouth with the back of his hand. 'He remains a powerful gentleman, does our Sir Money.'

Guadalmedina looked at him, surprised. 'Very well put. You should write a poem about it.'

'I have.'

'Really? Well, I'm pleased.'

'In the Indies he was born an honest man . . .' Don Francisco began, taking another sip of wine and reciting in a resonant voice.

'Oh, that,' said the Count, winking at Alatriste. 'I thought that was by Góngora.'

The poet choked on his wine. 'God's teeth and blood!'

'All right, my friend, all right . . .'

'No, Devil take it, it's not all right. Not even a Lutheran could come up with a worse insult. What have I got to do with poetasters and versifiers like him who in one bound go from being Jews or Moors to writing about innocent shepherds and shepherdesses?'

'It was only a joke.'

58

'I've had duels before now over jokes like that, Count.'

'Well, don't even consider such a possibility with me,' said the Count, smiling, conciliatory and good-natured, stroking his curled moustache and his goatee beard. 'I still remember the fencing lesson you gave to Pacheco de Narváez.' He gracefully raised his right hand and politely doffed an imaginary hat. 'My apologies, Don Francisco.'

'Hm.'

'What do you mean "Hm"? I'm a grandee of Spain, damn it! At least be so kind as to acknowledge my gesture.'

'Hm.'

Once the poet's wounded feelings had, despite everything, been soothed, Guadalmedina continued to provide more details to which Captain Alatriste listened intently, his mug of wine in his hand and his reddish profile half-lit by the flames of the candles on the table. At least war is clean, he had once said, some time ago. And at that moment I understood precisely what he meant. Foreigners, Guadalmedina was saying, got round the trading monopoly by using local intermediaries and third parties – they were called 'dodgers', a word that said it all – thus diverting the merchandise, the gold and the silver, which they would never have been able to obtain directly. More to the point, the idea that the galleons left Seville and returned there was a legal fiction; they almost always remained moored in Cádiz, in El Puerto de Santa

María or Barra de Sanlúcar, where the cargo was loaded onto another ship. This encouraged many merchants to move into that area, since it was easier to elude the guards there.

'They've even built ships with an official declared tonnage but whose real tonnage is quite different. Everyone knows that while they happily own up to carrying five tons they can, in fact, carry ten. Bribery and corruption, however, keep people's mouths shut and their willingness to co-operate open. A great many people have made their fortune that way.' Guadalmedina studied the bowl of his pipe as if its contents merited his particular attention. 'And that includes certain high-up royal officials.'

Guadalmedina continued his account. Made lethargic by the benefits of overseas trade, Seville like the rest of Spain had become incapable of sustaining any industry of its own. Many people from other lands had managed to set up businesses there and, thanks to their hard work and tenacity, had made themselves indispensable. This put them in a privileged position as intermediaries between Spain and the parts of Europe with which we were at war. The paradox was that while we were locked in battle with England, France and Denmark, as well as with the Turks and the rebel provinces, we were at the same time, through those intermediaries, buying all kinds of merchandise from them: rigging, tar, sails and other goods that were essential both in the Peninsula and across the Atlantic.

60

Thus the gold from the Indies slipped away to finance the armies and navies that were fighting us. It was an open secret, but no one put a stop to this traffic because everyone was profiting from it. Including the King.

'The result is obvious: Spain is going to the dogs. Everyone steals, cheats and lies, and no one pays their debts.'

'They even boast about it,' added Quevedo.

'They do.'

The smuggling of gold and silver, Guadalmedina went on, was crucial to this state of affairs. With the frequent connivance of customs officers and officials at the Casa de Contratación, only half the real value of any treasure imported by individuals was declared. Each fleet brought with it a fortune that disappeared into private pockets or ended up in London, Amsterdam, Paris or Genoa. This smuggling was enthusiastically embraced by foreigners and Spaniards alike, by merchants, government officials, captains of fleets, admirals, passengers, sailors, soldiers and clerics. An example of the latter was Bishop Pérez de Espinosa, who, when he died in Seville a couple of years earlier, had left five hundred thousand reals and sixty-two gold ingots, which were immediately seized by the Crown when it was discovered that all this wealth had come from the Indies without having passed through customs.

'It's estimated,' Guadalmedina went on, 'that, taking into account the King's treasure and that brought in by private individuals, the treasure fleet

61

which is about to arrive is carrying – along with sundry other merchandise – twenty million silver reals from Zacatecas and Potosí as well as eighty quintals of gold in bars.'

'And that's only the official amount,' said Quevedo.

'Exactly. They reckon that of the silver a quarter more is arriving as contraband. As for the gold, it almost all belongs to the royal treasury, but one of the galleons is carrying a secret cargo of ingots that no one has declared.'

The Count paused and took a long drink so as to allow Captain Alatriste to absorb these facts. Quevedo had taken out a small box containing powdered tobacco. He took a pinch and, after sneezing discreetly, wiped his nose on the crumpled handkerchief he kept up his sleeve.

'The ship is called the *Virgen de Regla*,' Guadalmedina continued at last. 'It's a sixteen-cannon galleon, the property of the Duke of Medina Sidonia and hired by a Genoese merchant based in Seville called Jerónimo Garaffa. On the voyage out it transports a variety of goods – from Almadén mercury for the silver mines to papal bulls – and on the return voyage it carries everything and anything it can. And it can carry a great deal because, while its official capacity is nine hundred barrels of twenty-seven *arrobas* each, in reality it has been built so that its actual capacity is one thousand four hundred barrels . . .'

The *Virgen de Regla*, he went on, was travelling with the treasure fleet, and its declared cargo included liquid amber, cochineal, wool and skins intended for the merchants of Cádiz and Seville. There were also five million silver reals – two thirds of which were the property of private individuals – and one thousand five hundred gold ingots destined for the royal treasury.

'A fine booty for pirates,' commented Quevedo.

'Especially when you consider that this year's fleet comprises another four ships with similar cargo.' Guadalmedina studied the captain through his pipe smoke. 'Now do you understand why the English were so interested in Cádiz?'

'And how did the English know?'

'Damn it, Alatriste. *We* know, don't we? If you can buy the salvation of your soul with money, imagine what else you can buy. You seem a touch ingenuous tonight, Alatriste. Where have you spent the last few years? In Flanders or in limbo?'

Alatriste poured himself more wine and said nothing. His eyes rested on Quevedo, who gave a faint smile and shrugged. That's the way it is, said the gesture. And always has been.

'At any rate,' Guadalmedina was saying, 'it doesn't much matter what they claim the official cargo to be. We know that the galleon is also carrying contraband silver at an estimated value of one million reals. The silver, however, is the least of it. The *Virgen de Regla* is carrying in its hold another two thousand gold bars – undeclared.' The Count pointed with the stem of his pipe at the captain. 'Do you know how much that secret cargo is worth, at the very lowest estimate?'

'I haven't the slightest idea.'

'Well, it's worth two hundred thousand gold escudos.'

The captain was studying his hands, which lay motionless on the table. He was calculating. 'That's one hundred million *maravedís*,' he murmured.

'Exactly.' Guadalmedina was laughing. 'Everyone knows how much an escudo is worth.'

Alatriste looked up and stared hard at the Count.

'You're mistaken there,' he said. 'Not everyone knows it as well as I do.'

Guadalmedina opened his mouth, doubtless intending to make some new joke, but the icy expression on my master's face immediately dissuaded him. We knew that Captain Alatriste had killed men for a tiny fraction of that amount. He was doubtless imagining, as was I, how many armies could be bought for such a sum. How many harquebuses, how many lives and how many deaths. How many minds and how many consciences.

Quevedo cleared his throat and then recited in a low voice:

> *'Life and stealing are the same,*
> *Thieving is no deadly vice,*
> *All that's worldly has a price,*
> *So take it, filch it, that's the game.*
> *None is ever stripped and whipped*

For stealing silver, gold or cash;
The poor, alone, deserve the lash.'

This was followed by an awkward silence. The Count's gaze was fixed on his pipe. Finally, he put it down on the table.

'In order to carry those forty quintals of extra gold, as well as the undeclared silver,' he went on, 'the captain of the *Virgen de Regla* has removed eight of the galleon's cannon. They say that even so she's still very heavily laden.'

'Who does the gold belong to?'

'That's a delicate matter. On the one hand, there's the Duke of Medina Sidonia, who is organising the whole operation, providing the ship and creaming off the largest profit. There's also a banker in Lisbon and another in Antwerp, and then a few people at Court. One of them, it seems, is the royal secretary, Luis de Alquézar.'

The captain shot me a glance. I had of course told him of my encounter with Gualterio Malatesta outside the royal palace, although I had made no mention of the carriage and the blue eyes I thought I had glimpsed in the Queen's retinue. Guadalmedina and Quevedo, who were in turn watching the captain, exchanged a look.

'The plan,' said the Count, 'is this. Before unloading officially in Cádiz or Seville, the *Virgen de Regla* will anchor at Barra de Sanlúcar. The captain and the admiral of the fleet have both been bribed to anchor the ships there for at least one night on the pretext of bad weather or the English or some other excuse. The contraband gold will be transferred to another galleon waiting there – the *Niklaasbergen*, a Flemish *urca* from Ostend with an irreproachably Catholic captain, crew and owner, which is free to come and go between Spain and Flanders under the protection of our King's flag.'

'Where will the gold be taken?'

'Medina Sidonia's share and that of the other individuals will go to Lisbon, where the Portuguese banker will keep it in a safe place. The rest will be sent straight to the rebel provinces.'

'That's treason,' said Alatriste.

His voice was quite calm, and the hand that raised his mug to his lips, wetting his moustache with wine, remained perfectly steady, but I saw his pale eyes grow strangely dark.

'Treason,' he said again.

The tone in which he said the word revived recent memories. The ranks of the Spanish infantry standing undaunted on the plain surrounding the Ruyter mill, with the drums beating at our backs awakening a nostalgia for Spain in those about to die. The good *gallego* Rivas and the ensign Chacón, who had died trying to save the blue and white chequered flag beside the Terheyden redoubt. The cry from a hundred men as they emerged at dawn from the canals for the assault on Oudkerk. The soldiers whose eyes were gritty with dirt after fighting

66

hand to hand in the narrow mines and counter-mines. Suddenly, I too felt a desire to drink and I downed my mug of wine in one.

Quevedo and Guadalmedina exchanged another look.

'That's how Spain is, Captain Alatriste,' said Don Francisco. 'You seem to have forgotten that during your time in Flanders.'

'It's a purely commercial matter,' explained Guadalmedina. 'And this certainly isn't the first time it's happened. The only difference now is that the King, and even more so Olivares, both distrust Medina Sidonia. The welcome they received two years ago on his estate in Doña Ana and the lavish hospitality bestowed on them during this present visit make it clear that Don Manuel de Guzmán, the eighth duke, has become a little king of Andalusia. From Huelva to Málaga to Seville his word is law, and that, together with the Moor just across the water, and with Catalonia and Portugal being held together with pins, makes for a highly dangerous situation. Olivares fears that Medina Sidonia and his son Gaspar, the Count of Niebla, are preparing to give the Crown a real fright. Normally these things would be resolved by holding a trial in keeping with their social status and then slitting their throats. The Medina Sidonia family, however, is very high up the scale, and Olivares – who, despite being a relative of theirs, loathes them – would never dare involve their name in a public scandal without solid proof.'

'And what about Alquézar?'

'Not even the royal secretary is easy prey now. He has prospered at Court: he has the support of the Inquisitor Bocanegra and of the Council of Aragon. Besides, Olivares, with his dangerous taste for double-dealing, considers him to be useful.' Guadalmedina gave a scornful shrug. 'And so he has opted for a discreet and effective solution that will please everyone.'

'He is to be taught a lesson,' said Quevedo.

'Exactly. This includes snatching the contraband gold from beneath Medina Sidonia's nose and placing it instead in the royal coffers. Olivares has planned it all himself with the approval of the King, and that is the reason behind this royal visit to Seville. Our fourth Philip wishes to see the show himself and then, with his usual impassivity, to bid farewell to the old Duke by folding him in an embrace so tight that he'll be able to hear the Duke's teeth grinding. The problem is that the plan Olivares has come up with has two parts, one semi-official and somewhat delicate, and the other official and more . . . difficult.'

'The precise word is "dangerous",' said Quevedo, always exact when it came to language.

Guadalmedina leaned across the table towards the captain. 'As you will have gathered, the accountant Olmedilla is involved in the first part . . .'

My master nodded slowly. Now all the pieces were slotting into place. 'And I,' he said, 'am involved in the second'

Guadalmedina calmly stroked his moustache. He was smiling.

'That's what I like about you, Alatriste: there's never any need to explain things twice.'

It was already dark when we set off along the narrow ill-lit streets. The waning moon filled the entrance halls of the houses with a lovely milky light, bright enough for us to be able to see each other silhouetted beneath the eaves and the shady tops of the orange trees. Occasionally we passed dark shapes that scurried away when they saw us, for at that hour Seville was as dangerous as any other city. As we emerged into a small square a figure swathed in a cloak and leaning by a window, whispering, suddenly drew back and the window slammed shut, and in the black masculine shadow we could see a precautionary glint of steel. Guadalmedina gave a reassuring laugh, bade the motionless figure, 'Goodnight,' and we continued on our way. The sound of our footsteps preceded us down alleyways and along the paths around the city walls. Now and then the light from an oil lamp could be seen through the shutters behind the grilles at windows, and candles or cheap tin lanterns burned at the corners of certain streets beneath images made from glazed tiles of Our Lady or of Christ in torment.

As we walked Guadalmedina explained that the accountant Olmedilla might be a mere faceless official, a creature of figures and files, but he had

69

a real talent for his job. He enjoyed the complete confidence of the Count-Duke of Olivares, whom he advised on all accounting matters. And just so that we could get an idea of his character, he added that Olmedilla had acted not only in the investigation that had led Rodrigo Calderón to the scaffold but also in the cases brought against the Dukes of Lerma and Osuna. More than that, he was held to be an honest man, something almost unheard of in his profession. His sole passions were addition, subtraction, multiplication and division, and the one goal of his life was to make the books balance. All the information they had received about the contraband gold came from reports compiled by the Count-Duke's spies, and these had been confirmed by several months of patient research by Olmedilla in the relevant offices, cabinets and archives.

'All that remains for us now is to ascertain the final details,' concluded the Count. 'The fleet has been sighted, and so we do not have much time. Everything has to be resolved tomorrow during a visit that Olmedilla will pay to Garaffa, the man who chartered the galleon, so that he can clarify certain points concerning the transfer of the gold to the *Niklaasbergen*. The visit is of course an unofficial one, and Olmedilla has no document or letter of authority.' Guadalmedina raised his eyebrows ironically. 'So Garaffa will probably refuse to talk.'

We passed a tavern. The window was lit and

from inside came the strumming of a guitar. A gust of laughter and singing emerged as the door opened. On the threshold a man vomited loudly before staggering homewards to sleep off the wine he had drunk. Between retches, we heard his hoarse cries invoking God, although not exactly in a spirit of prayerfulness.

'Why don't you just arrest this Garaffa?' asked Alatriste. 'A dungeon, a scribe and a bit of strappado can work wonders. All you have to do is call on the King's authority.'

'It's not that easy. There's a dispute over who holds sway in Seville, whether it's the Audiencia Real or the Cabildo, and the Archbishop has a finger in every pie. Garaffa is well connected with the Church and with Medina Sidonia. There would be a huge scandal and meanwhile the gold would vanish. No, everything must be done as discreetly as possible. And once Garaffa has told us what he knows, he will have to disappear for a few days. He lives alone with just the one servant, so no one would mind very much if he disappeared for ever.' He paused significantly. 'Not even the King.'

After saying this, Guadalmedina walked a little way in silence. Quevedo was lagging slightly behind me, limping along in his dignified fashion, one hand on my shoulder as if, in a way, he were trying to keep me out of the whole business.

'In short, Alatriste, it's up to you how you play the cards.'

I couldn't see the captain's face, only his dark silhouette ahead of me, his hat and the tip of his sword, which glinted in the rectangles of moonlight that slipped through the gaps between the eaves. After a moment, I heard him say, 'Getting rid of the Genoese gentleman is easy enough, but as for the other business . . .'

He paused, then stood still. We caught up with him. He had his head slightly bowed, and when he looked up his pale eyes glittered in the darkness.

'I don't like torturing people.'

He said this quite simply, bluntly and without drama. An objective fact spoken out loud. He didn't like sour wine either, or stew with too much salt in it, or men who were incapable of sticking to the rules, even if those rules were personal, individual and apparently unimportant. There was a silence, and Quevedo removed his hand from my shoulder. Guadalmedina gave an awkward little cough.

'That's none of my business,' he said at last, somewhat embarrassed. 'Nor do I wish to know anything about it. How you get the information we need is a matter for Olmedilla and for you. He does his job and you get paid for helping him.'

'Besides, dealing with Garaffa is the easy part,' said Quevedo in a placatory tone.

'It is,' agreed Guadalmedina, 'because once Garaffa has given us the final details of the plan, there is another minor matter, Alatriste.'

He was standing opposite the captain, and any awkwardness he may have felt before had vanished. I couldn't see his face clearly, but I'm sure he was smiling.

'The accountant Olmedilla will provide you with money to recruit a select group of men – old friends and so on . . . professional swordsmen, to put it bluntly. The best you can find.'

There came the sing-song voice of a beggar standing at the end of the street, an oil lamp in his hand, calling on us to pray for the souls in Purgatory. 'Remember the dead,' he was saying. 'Remember.' Guadalmedina watched the light from the lamp until it was swallowed up by the darkness, and then he turned again to my master. 'Then you will have to board that wretched Flemish ship.'

Still talking, we reached the part of the city wall near El Arenal, by the little archway known as El Golpe, with its image of the Virgin of Atocha on the whitewashed wall above. El Golpe provided access to the famous Compás de la Laguna bawdy house. When the gates of Triana and El Arenal were closed, that archway and the bawdy house became the easiest way to slip out of the city. And, as he had hinted to us, Guadalmedina had an important appointment in Triana, at La Gamarra tavern, on the other side of the pontoon bridge that linked the two banks of the river. La Gamarra stood next to a convent whose nuns had all reputedly been sent there against their will. The Sunday morning mass attracted even larger crowds than the latest play at the playhouse and it positively seethed with people; there were wimples and white hands on one side of the grille and young men sighing on the other. And, or so people said, such was the fervour of certain gentlemen from the best society – including distinguished strangers to the city, such as our King – they even came to worship there during the hours of darkness.

As for the bawdy house, a popular expression of the day, '*más puta que la Méndez*' – more of a whore than La Méndez herself – referred to a real woman whose name had been used by Don Francisco de Quevedo in his famous ballads about a celebrated figure from the criminal classes called Escarramán, as well as by other men of letters. She had worked as a prostitute in the bawdy house, which offered the travellers and merchants staying in nearby Calle de Tintores and in other city inns, as well as the locals, gaming, music and women of the kind described by the great Lope de Vega thus:

How foolish, how mad of a silly young man
To chase, helter-skelter (how he pants and drools),
After one of those women who've already been
Bait to a thousand other young fools.

And which the no less great Don Francisco had finished off in his own inimitable style:

74

Stupid the man who trusts in whores
And stupid the man who wants them;
Stupid the money handed over
To pay for whorish flotsam.

Stupid the desire, stupid the delight
The whorish moment imparts,
And stupid the man who doesn't believe –
Madam, you're the queen of tarts!

The bawdy house was run by one Garciposadas, from a family notorious in Seville for two of its brothers: one was a poet at court – a friend of Góngora's, as it happened, who had been burned that very year for sodomising a mulatto, Pepillo Infante, also a poet and a servant of the Admiral of Castile. The other brother had been burned three years before in Málaga as a Judaiser, and since misfortunes always come in threes, these antecedents had earned Garciposadas the nickname of *el Tostao*, or Garciposadas the Scorched. This worthy fellow performed the duties of pimp or father of the bawdy house with great aplomb: he kept the authorities suitably lubricated to ensure that his business ran smoothly, and so as not to contravene the regulations laid down by the city's *corregidor*, or governor, he always ensured that weapons of any kind were deposited in the hallway and forbade entry to any customers under the age of fourteen. The said Garciposadas was also on good terms with the constables and catchpoles, who quite blatantly protected him and his business, a situation that can be aptly summed up in these words:

I am both innocent and devious,
Naive and promiscuous;
Rile me, yet my wrath is soothed
With a small reward, however lewd.

The reward in question was of course a nice fat purse. The place was always packed with petty criminals: rogues who swore upon the soul of Escamilla, scoundrels and rascals from La Heria, dealers in lives and purveyors of stab wounds. It was a picturesque pot, spiced with ruined aristocrats, idle New World nabobs, bourgeois gentlemen with plenty of cash, clerics in disguise, gamblers, pimps, informers, swindlers and individuals of every kind, some with noses so keen they could smell a stranger a harquebus shot away, and who were often perfectly safe from a justice, of which Don Francisco de Quevedo himself wrote:

Sevillean justice can prove scarce,
For the length of sentence handed out
Depends on the size of your purse.

Thus each night, under the protection of the authorities, El Compás enjoyed a constant flow of people, a secular feast where only the finest wines were served and those who went in as sober friends

76

came out as wine-soaked sots. There they danced the lascivious *zarabanda*, guitar strings were plucked and so were clients, and everyone did as they pleased. The bawdy house was home to thirty sirens whose singing emptied men's purses; each of these sirens had her own room, and every Saturday morning – for people of quality visited El Compás on Saturday night – a constable would visit to make sure that none of the girls was infected with the French disease and would not therefore give her clients cause to curse and swear, and leave them wondering why God hadn't given the Turk and the Lutheran what he had given them. They say the Archbishop was in despair, for as one can read in a memoir of the time: 'What one finds most in Seville is men and women living in sin, false witnesses, rogues, murderers and opportunists. There are more than 300 gaming dens and 3,000 prostitutes.'

But to return to our story – which does not involve a long journey – the fact is that, as ill luck would have it, just as Guadalmedina was about to bid us farewell underneath the archway of El Golpe, almost at the entrance to the bawdy house, a patrol of catchpoles led by a constable with his staff of office passed by. You will recall that the incident of the hanged soldier days before had caused hostilities to break out between the law and soldiers from the galleys, and both parties were looking for revenge, which is why, during the day, there wasn't a law officer to be seen on the streets and why, at night, the soldiers took care to stay outside the city, in Triana.

'Well, well, well,' said the constable when he saw us.

Guadalmedina, Quevedo, the captain and myself exchanged bewildered glances. It was equally ill luck that, of all the riff-raff coming and going in the shadow of the bawdy house, that particular brooch and all his pins should have chosen to stick themselves into us.

'Out taking the cool air, are we, gentlemen?' added the constable scornfully.

His bravado was backed up by his four men, who were armed with swords, shields and black looks which the dim light made blacker still. Then I understood. By the light of the lantern of the Virgin of Atocha, the clothes worn by Captain Alatriste and Guadalmedina, and even by me, made us look like soldiers. Guadalmedina's buff coat was forbidden in time of peace – ironically enough he had probably worn it that night in his role as the King's escort – and Captain Alatriste of course was the very image of the military man. Quevedo, as quick-thinking as ever, saw the problem coming and tried to put things right.

'Forgive me, sir,' he said very courteously to the constable, 'but I can assure you that we are all honourable men.'

A few curious onlookers gathered round to see what was happening: a couple of whores, a rogue or two and a drunk who was already several sheets to the wind. Even Garciposadas himself peered out from beneath the arch. This small crowd emboldened the constable.

'And who asked you to tell us something we can find out for ourselves?'

I heard Guadalemedina tut-tutting impatiently. 'Don't back down now,' said an encouraging voice from among the shadows and the throng of inquisitive lookers-on. There was laughter too. More people were gathering underneath the arch. Some took the side of the law and others, the majority, urged us to catch as many catchpoles as we could.

'I arrest you in the name of the King.'

This did not augur well. Guadalmedina and Quevedo looked at each other, and I saw the Count wrap his cloak round his body and over his shoulder, revealing his sword arm and his sword but taking care to cover his face.

'It is not the custom of the well born to suffer such outrages,' he said.

'I don't care two figs whether it is or not,' retorted the constable in surly tones.

With this refined remark the scene was set. As for my master, he remained very still and quiet, studying the constable and his companions, the catchpoles. He cut an imposing figure in the half-light, with his aquiline profile and his bushy moustache beneath the broad brim of his hat. Or rather so it seemed to me, who knew him well. I touched the hilt of my dagger. I would have given anything for a sword, because there were five of them and we were only four. I immediately and regretfully corrected myself. With my few inches of steel, we were really only three and a half.

'Hand over your swords,' said the constable, 'and be so good as to come with us.'

'These are important people,' Quevedo said in one last attempt to save the situation.

'Right, and I'm the Duke of Alba.'

It was clear that the constable was determined to have his way, and to force two and two to make five if necessary. This was his parish, and he was being watched by his parishioners. The four catchpoles unsheathed their swords and spread out to form a wide semicircle around us.

'If we get out of this alive and no one identifies us,' Guadalmedina whispered coolly, his voice muffled behind his cloak, 'that will be that, but if not, gentlemen, the nearest church in which to seek sanctuary is San Francisco.'

The constable and his men were getting closer. In their black clothes the catchpoles merged with the shadows. Underneath the arch, the bystanders urged them on with mocking applause. 'Go on, teach 'em a lesson, Sánchez,' someone said to the constable in a bantering tone. Unhurriedly, confidently and boldly, the said Sánchez stuck his staff of office in his belt, grasped his sword in his right hand and brandished a huge pistol in his left.

'I'll count to three,' he said, coming closer. 'One . . .'

Don Francisco de Quevedo pushed me gently

80

behind him, interposing himself between the catchpoles and me. Guadalmedina was watching Captain Alatriste, who was still standing impassively in the same place, judging distances and turning his body very slowly so as not to lose sight of the face of the catchpole nearest to him but still keeping an eye on the others. I noticed that Guadalmedina was checking to see who my master was looking at, and then, turning away, he fixed on another as if satisfied that my master would deal with the first man.

'Two . . .'

Quevedo was removing his short cape. 'There's nothing for it, et cetera, et cetera,' he muttered as he undid the fastening and wrapped the cloth around his left arm. Guadalmedina, for his part, had arranged his cloak so as to protect his torso from the knife-thrusts that were about to rain down upon him. I stepped away from Quevedo and went to stand next to the captain. His right hand was moving towards the guard of his sword and the left was resting on the hilt of his dagger. I could hear his slow steady breathing. I realised suddenly that I had not seen him kill a man for several months, not since Breda.

'Three,' said the constable, raising his pistol and glancing back at the onlookers. 'In the name of the King and of the law—'

He had not even finished speaking when Guadalmedina fired one of his pistols at point-blank range, which sent the constable reeling back, his face still turned away. A woman underneath the archway screamed, and an expectant murmur ran through the shadows, for the spectacle of fellow Spaniards quarrelling and knifing each other has long been a popular Spanish sport. And then, as one, Quevedo, Alatriste and Guadalmedina reached for their blades; seven bare lengths of steel glinted in the street, and then everything happened with diabolical speed: *cling, clang*, sparks flying, catchpoles shouting, 'Stop in the name of the King!' and more cries and murmurs from the spectators. I too had unsheathed my dagger, though I did nothing with it, for in less time than it takes to say an Ave Maria, Guadalmedina had skewered the upper arm of one catchpole, Quevedo had slashed the face of another, leaving him leaning against the wall, hands pressed to the wound and bleeding like a stuck pig, and Alatriste, sword in one hand and dagger in the other, wielding both as if they were bolts of lightning, had put two spans of Toledan steel through the chest of a third, who cried out, 'Holy Mother of God!' before detaching himself from the blade and falling to the ground, vomiting gobbets of blood as dark as black ink. It all happened so fast that the fourth catchpole didn't think twice and took to his heels when my master rounded on him as his next victim. At that point I sheathed my dagger and went over to pick up one of the swords lying on the ground, the constable's sword, and as I did so two or three of the onlookers who had misread the situation at the start stepped forward to come to the aid of the catchpoles. However, when they saw how quickly everything had been resolved, they stopped short and stood very still and circumspect, watching the captain, Guadalmedina and Quevedo, who now turned on them with their naked blades, ready to continue their harvest. I took up a position beside my companions and placed myself on guard, and the hand that held the sword was trembling not with anxiety but with excitement: I would have given anything to have contributed a sword thrust of my own to the fight. However, the would-be combatants from the small crowd were fast losing their desire to join in. Prudently they hung back, muttering this and that – let's just wait and see, eh – while the other onlookers jeered at them and we walked slowly backwards away from the scene, leaving the street bathed in blood: one catchpole dead, the constable with his pistol wound more dead than alive and with not even enough breath to call for a confessor, the one with the cut to his arm staunching the wound as best he could, and the man with the slashed face kneeling by the wall moaning behind a mask of blood.

'They'll tell you where to find us on the King's galleys!' cried Guadalmedina in a suitably defiant tone as we dodged round the nearest corner. This was a clever ploy on his part, for it would place the blame for that night's fighting on the soldiers whom the constable had, to his cost, believed us to be.

The constable and his catchpoles
Were eager for the kill,
But I taught those turds a lesson
And one was sent to Hell.

As we strolled along Calle de Harinas towards the gate of El Arenal Don Francisco de Quevedo was making up a few more scatological lines of poetry, all the while looking out for a tavern where he could toast both his poetry and us with some good wine. Guadalmedina was laughing, delighted with the whole business. An excellent move and very well played, damn it! Captain Alatriste meanwhile had cleaned the blade of his sword with a kerchief he kept in his pouch, and when he had replaced his sword in its sheath walked on in silence, occupied with thoughts impossible to penetrate. And I walked along beside him, carrying the constable's sword and feeling as proud as Don Quijote.

CHAPTER 4

THE QUEEN'S MAID OF HONOUR

D iego Alatriste was waiting, leaning against a wall, amongst pots of geraniums and basil, in the shade of a porch in Calle del Mesón del Moro. Without his cloak but with his hat on, sword and dagger in his belt and doublet open over a clean neatly darned shirt, he was intently watching the house of the Genoese merchant Garaffa. The house was almost at the gates of the old Jewish quarter in Seville, near the convent of the Discalced Carmelites and the old Doña Elvira playhouse, and it was very quiet at that hour, with few passers-by and only the occasional woman sweeping the entrance to her house or watering her plants. In earlier days, when he was serving as a soldier on the King's galleys, Alatriste had often visited that quarter, never imagining that, later on, when he returned from Italy in the year 1616, he would spend a long time there, most of it in the company of ruffians and other people quick to draw their swords, in the famous cathedral court-yard, the Corral de los Naranjos, which was a meeting place for the boldest and most cunning of Seville's criminal class. After the repression of the

Moriscos in Valencia, as you may perhaps remember, the captain had asked if he could leave his regiment in order to enlist as a soldier in Naples – 'where,' he reasoned, 'if I have to slit the throats of infidels, they will at least be able to defend them-selves' – and he remained embarked until the naval battle of 1615, when, following a devastating raid on the Turkish coast with five galleys and more than a thousand comrades, he and his fellow soldiers had returned to Italy with plenty of plunder, and he was able to lead a life of pleasure in Naples. This ended as such things tend to end in youth, with a woman and another man, with a mark on the face for the woman and a sword thrust for the man, and with Diego Alatriste fleeing Naples thanks to the help of his old friend Captain Don Alonso de Contreas, who stowed him away on a galley bound for Sanlúcar and Seville. And that was how, before he moved on to Madrid, this former soldier had come to earn his living as a paid swordsman in Seville, that Babylon and breeding ground for all vices, taking refuge by day among ruffians and scoundrels in the famous cathedral courtyard and by night sallying forth to carry out the duties of his profession, one in which any man with courage and a good sword, and with sufficient luck and skill, could easily earn his daily bread. Such legendary ruffians as Gonzalo Xeniz, Gayoso, Ahumada and the great Pedro Vázquez de Escamilla – who only recognised one kind of king, the king in the deck of cards – were all long gone, undone by a knife

86

thrust or by the disease of the noose, for in work such as theirs finding oneself strung up by the neck was a highly contagious complaint. However, in the Corral de los Naranjos and in the royal prison, where he also took up temporary residence with some regularity, Alatriste had met many a worthy successor to such historic rogues, experts in how to stab, cut and slash, although he too soon made a name for himself in that illustrious brotherhood, skilled as he was in the sword-thrust perfected by the celebrated ruffian Gayona, as well as in many others proper to his art.

He was recalling all of this now with a pang of nostalgia, less perhaps for the past than for his lost youth, and he was doing so not a stone's throw from the very playhouse where as a young man he had grown to love the plays of Lope, Tirso de Molina and others – it was there he saw for the first time *The Dog in the Manger* and *The Shy Man at the Palace* – on nights that opened with poetry and staged fights and closed with taverns, wine, complaisant whores, jolly companions and knives. This dangerous fascinating Seville still existed, and any change was to be sought not in the city but in himself. *Time does not pass in vain,* he thought as he stood leaning in the shady porch. *And a man grows old inside, just as his heart does.*

'Death and damnation, Captain Alatriste, but it's a small world!'

The captain spun round in surprise to see who it was that had spoken his name. It was strange to see Sebastián Copons so far from a Flemish trench and uttering more than eight words together. It took the captain a few seconds to return to the very recent past: the sea voyage, his recent farewell to Copons in Cádiz, the latter's intention to spend a few days' leave there and then to travel up to Seville on his way north.

'It's good to see you, Sebastián.'

This was both true and not true. It was not in fact good to see him at that precise moment, and while they clasped each other's arms with the sober affection of two old comrades Alatriste glanced over Copons' shoulder towards the far end of the street. Fortunately, Copons could be relied on, and Alatriste could get rid of him without causing offence, knowing that he would understand. That after all was the good thing about a real friend: he trusted you to deal the cards fairly and never insisted on checking the deck.

'Are you stopping in Seville?' he asked.

'For a while.'

Copons, small, thin and wiry, was dressed as ever in soldier's garb, in jerkin, baldric, sword and boots. Beneath his hat, on his left temple, was the scar left by the gash that Alatriste himself had bandaged a year ago during the battle at Ruyter mill.

'How about a drink to celebrate, Diego?'

'Later.'

Copons looked at him, surprised and intrigued,

before half-turning to follow the direction of Alatriste's gaze.

'You're busy.'

'Something like that.'

Copons again inspected the street, searching for clues as to what was keeping his comrade there. Then, instinctively, he touched the hilt of his sword.

'Do you need me?' he asked phlegmatically.

'Not right now,' replied Alatriste with a warm smile that wrinkled his weathered face. 'But there might be something for you before you leave Seville. Would you be interested?'

'Are you in on it?'

'Yes, and it's well paid too.'

'I'd do it even if it weren't.'

At this point Alatriste spotted the accountant Olmedilla at the end of the street. He was dressed as always entirely in black, tightly buttoned up to his ruff and wearing a narrow-brimmed hat and the air of an anonymous government official straight from the Real Audiencia.

'I have to go, but meet me later at Becerra's.'

Placing one hand on his friend's shoulder he said nothing more, but with an apparent lack of concern crossed the street to join the accountant by the house on the corner, a two-storey brick building with a discreet gateway leading to an inner courtyard. They went in without knocking and without speaking to each other, exchanging only a brief knowing glance. Alatriste had his hand on the hilt of his sword and Olmedilla remained as sour-faced as ever. An elderly servant came into the courtyard, wiping his hands on his apron and looking anxious and inquisitive.

'We are here in the name of the Holy Office of the Inquisition,' said Olmedilla with terrible coldness.

The servant's expression changed, for in Garaffa's house and indeed in the whole of Seville these were not words to be taken lightly. And so when Alatriste, one hand still on the hilt of his sword, indicated a room, the servant entered it as meekly as a lamb, allowing himself without a murmur of protest to be bound and gagged and locked in. When Alatriste came back out, he found Olmedilla waiting behind an enormous potted fern, twiddling his thumbs impatiently. There was another silent exchange of glances, and the two men went across the courtyard to a closed door. Then Alatriste unsheathed his sword, flung open the door and strode into a spacious study furnished with a desk, a cupboard, a copper brazier and a few leather chairs. The light from a high barred window, half-covered by latticework shutters, cast innumerable tiny luminous squares onto the head and shoulders of a stout middle-aged man dressed in a silk robe and slippers, who started to his feet. This time Olmedilla did not invoke the Holy Office or anything else; he merely followed Alatriste into the room and after a quick look around his eyes alighted with professional satisfaction on the open cupboard stuffed with papers. Just the way a cat would have licked its lips at the sight of a sardine placed half an inch from its whiskers, thought the Captain. As for the owner of the house, Jerónimo Garaffa, all the blood seemed to have drained from his face; he stood quietly, his mouth agape, both hands resting on the table on which a sealing-wax candle was burning. As he stood up he had spilled half an inkwell over the paper on which he had been writing when the intruders burst in. His dyed hair was covered by a snood and his waxed moustache by a net. He continued to hold a pen between his fingers as if he had forgotten it was there, transfixed in horror by the sword Captain Alatriste was now pressing to his throat.

'So you have no idea what we're talking about.'

The accountant Olmedilla, as comfortably ensconced behind the desk as if he were in his own office, briefly raised his eyes from the papers to see Jerónimo Garaffa, still with his snood on, anxiously shaking his head. He was sitting on a chair, his hands tied to the chair back. It was not particularly warm in the room, but large beads of sweat were already running from his hair into his side whiskers, and his face smelled of gum arabic, collyria and barber's lotions.

'I swear to you, sir—'

Olmedilla interrupted this protest with an abrupt wave of his hand and resumed his scrutiny

of the documents before him. Above the moustache net, which gave his face the grotesque
appearance of a carnival mask, Garaffa's eyes
turned to rest on Diego Alatriste, who was listening
in silence, leaning against the wall, sword sheathed,
arms folded. The man must have found Alatriste's
icy eyes more troubling even than Olmedilla's
abrupt manner, for he turned back to the accountant
like someone forced to choose the lesser of two
evils. After a long oppressive silence, the accountant
abandoned the documents he was studying, sat
back in his chair, hands clasped and, again twiddling his thumbs, stared at Garaffa. It seemed to
Alatriste that he looked even more the part of
the grey government mouse, except that his
expression was now that of a mouse with bad
indigestion who keeps swallowing bile.

'Let's get this quite straight,' said Olmedilla
coldly and deliberately. 'You know what I'm
talking about and we know that you know.
Everything else is a pure waste of time.'

Garaffa's mouth was so dry it took him three
attempts before he could articulate a word.

'I swear by Christ Our Lord,' he said in a hoarse
voice, his foreign accent made more marked by
fear, 'that I know nothing about this Flemish ship.'

'Christ has nothing to do with it!'

'This is an outrage. I demand justice . . .'

Garaffa's final attempt to give some substance
to his protest ended in a sob. The mere sight of
Diego Alatriste's face told him that the justice to

which he was referring – and which he was doubt-less accustomed to buying with a few lovely pieces of eight – only existed somewhere far away from that room and that there was no help to be had.

'Where will the *Virgen de Regla* anchor?' asked Olmedilla very quietly.

'I don't know . . . Holy Mother of God, I swear I don't know what you're talking about.'

The accountant nonchalantly scratched his nose. He gave Alatriste a significant look, and the captain thought to himself that Olmedilla really was the very image of Habsburg officialdom, always so meticu-lous and implacable with the unfortunate. He could as easily have been a judge, a scribe, a constable, a lawyer or any of the other insect life that lived and prospered under the protection of the monarchy. Guadalmedina and Quevedo had told him that Olmedilla was honest, and Alatriste believed them. As to his other qualities and attitudes, he was, Alatriste concluded, no different from the rabble of ruthless avaricious magpies that populated the courts and offices of lawyers and procurators, where – not even in one's dreams – would one find more arrogant Lucifers, more thievish Cacuses or more honour-greedy Tantaluses; no blasphemy uttered by an infidel could equal their decrees, which unfailingly favoured the powerful and damned the humble. They were, in short, loathsome blood-suckers who lacked all charity and decorum, but who brimmed with intemperance, acquisitiveness and the fanatical zeal of the hypocrite, so much so that the very people who were charged with protecting the poor and the destitute were precisely the ones voraciously tearing them apart with their greedy talons. However, the man in their grasp today did not quite fit that image. He was neither poor nor destitute, but he was certainly wretched.

'I see,' concluded Olmedilla.

He was tidying the papers on the desk, his eyes still trained on Alatriste as if signalling that he had nothing more to say. A few seconds passed, during which Olmedilla and the captain continued to observe each other in silence. Then the latter uncrossed his arms, abandoned his position by the wall and went over to Garaffa. By the time he reached Garaffa's side, the expression of terror on the merchant's face was indescribable. Alatriste stood in front of him, leaning slightly forward in order to fix his gaze more intensely. The man and everything he represented did not stir his reserves of pity in the least. Beneath the snood, the dyed hair was leaving trails of dark sweat on Garaffa's forehead and neck. Now, despite all the creams and pomades, he gave off a sour smell – of perspiration and fear.

'Jerónimo,' whispered Alatriste.

When he heard his name pronounced barely three inches from his face, Garaffa flinched as if he had been slapped. The captain did not draw back but remained for a few moments, motionless and silent, regarding him. His moustache was almost touching the prisoner's nose.

'I've seen a lot of men tortured,' he said at last, very slowly. 'With their arms and legs dislocated by the strappado. I've seen them betray their own children. I've seen renegades flayed alive, screaming and begging to be killed. In Valencia I saw poor Moorish converts having the soles of their feet burned to make them reveal where they'd hidden their gold while in the background they could hear the cries of their twelve-year-old daughters being raped by soldiers . . .'

He fell silent, as if he could go on listing such incidents indefinitely and there was therefore no point in continuing. Garaffa's face was as pale as if the hand of death had just passed over it. He had suddenly stopped sweating and beneath his skin, yellow with terror, it appeared that not one drop of blood flowed.

'Everyone talks sooner or later,' concluded the captain, 'or nearly everyone. Sometimes, if the torturer proves clumsy, the person dies first, but that wouldn't be the case with you.'

He remained a while longer staring at him, almost nose to nose, then went over to the desk. Standing there with his back to the prisoner, Alatriste rolled up the shirtsleeve on his left arm. While he was doing so his eye caught that of Olmedilla, who was watching intently, slightly perplexed. Then he picked up the sealing-wax candle and went back over to Garaffa. When he showed it to him, lifting it up a little, the light from the flame picked out the grey-green of his eyes, once more fixed on Garaffa like two slivers of ice.

'Watch,' he said.

He showed the merchant his forearm and the long slender scar which ran from wrist to elbow visible amongst the hairs. Then, right under the nose of the horrified Genoese, Captain Alatriste held the flame to his own bare skin. The flame crackled and there arose a smell of burnt flesh as the captain clenched his jaw and fist, and the tendons and muscles of his forearm grew as hard as vine shoots carved in stone. The captain's eyes remained green and impassive, but Garaffa's bulged in horror. This lasted for one long seemingly interminable moment. Then, very calmly, Alatriste put the candlestick down on the desk, returned to the prisoner and showed him his arm. A hideous burn the size of a silver piece of eight was reddening the scorched skin along the edges of the old wound.

'Jerónimo,' he said.

He again brought his face very close to Garaffa's and spoke to him in that same soft, almost confiding tone: 'If I can do this to myself, imagine what I would be capable of doing to you.'

A yellowish liquid emanating from the prisoner began to form a puddle around the legs of the chair. Garaffa started to moan and shake and did so for some time. When he finally recovered the power of speech, he let out a prodigious torrential stream of words, while Olmedilla diligently dipped his pen in the inkwell and made whatever

96

notes he deemed necessary. Alatriste went into the kitchen in search of some lard, grease or oil to apply to the burn. When he returned, bandaging his forearm with a clean piece of cloth, Olmedilla gave him a look which, in a man of a different temperament, would have been one of enormous respect. As for Garaffa, oblivious to everything but his own feelings of terror, he continued to gabble on and on, giving names, places, dates, details of Portuguese banks and gold bars.

At this same hour I was walking under the long vaulted passageway that leads from the Patio de Banderas into Callejón de la Aljama in what had once been the Jewish quarter. And, albeit for very different reasons from those of Jerónimo Garaffa, I too felt as if I had not one drop of blood in my veins. I stopped at the designated place and, fearing that my legs might give way beneath me, placed one hand on the wall to support myself. My instinct for self-preservation, however, had developed over the last few years and so, despite everything, I remained clear-headed enough to study the situation carefully – the two exits and those troubling little doors set into the walls. I touched the handle of my dagger, which I wore, as always, tucked into my belt at my back, and then I touched the pouch containing the note that had brought me here. It was worthy of a scene in a play by Tirso de Molina or Lope de Vega.

If you still care for me, now is the moment to prove it. I would like to meet you at eleven o'clock in the passageway leading to the Jewish quarter.

I had received this note at nine o'clock from a boy who came to the inn in Calle Tintores, where, seated on the little ledge by the door watching the people go by I awaited the captain's return. There was no signature, but the name of the sender was as clear to me as the deep wounds in my heart and my memory. You can imagine the conflicting feelings that troubled me following the receipt of that note and the delicious anxiety that guided my steps. I will not describe in detail all the anxieties of the lover, which would shame me and bore you, the reader. I will say only that I was sixteen years old then and had never loved a girl or a woman – nor did I love anyone afterwards – as I loved Angélica de Alquézar.

It really was most odd. I knew that the note could only be another episode in the dangerous game that Angélica had been playing with me ever since we first met outside the Inn of the Turk in Madrid. A game that had almost cost me my honour and my life and which, many times over the years, would cause me to walk along the very brink of the abyss, the deadly edge of the most delicious blade a woman was capable of creating for the man who, throughout her life and even at the very moment of her early death, would be

98

both her lover and her enemy. That moment, however, was still far off and there I was, on that mild winter morning in Seville, striding along with all the vigour and audacity of my youth to keep an appointment with the girl – perhaps not so much of a girl now, I thought – who once, almost three years before at the Fuente del Acero, had responded to my heartfelt 'I would die for you' with a sweet enigmatic smile and the words, 'Perhaps you will.'

The Arco de la Aljama was deserted. Leaving behind me the cathedral tower, which was silhouetted against the sky above the tops of the orange trees, I walked further along until I turned the corner and emerged on the other side, where the water in a fountain sang softly to itself and the thick twining branches of creepers hung down from the battlements of the Alcázares, the royal palace. There was no one there either. Perhaps it was all a joke, I thought, retracing my steps and plunging back into the shadows of the passageway. That was when I heard a noise behind me, and as I turned I put my hand on my dagger. One of the doors stood open, and a burly blond soldier in the German guard was observing me in silence. He gestured to me and I approached cautiously, fearing some trick, but the German appeared to be friendly. He was examining me with professional curiosity, and when I reached his side, he gestured again, this time indicating that I should surrender my dagger. Beneath the enormous fair side whiskers and moustache he wore a good-natured smile. Then he said something like '*Komensi herein*', which I – having seen more than enough Germans, alive and dead, in Flanders – knew to mean 'Come along' or 'Come in' or something of the sort. I had no choice, and so I handed him my dagger and went in through the door.

'Good morning, soldier.'

Anyone familiar with the portrait of Angélica Alquézar painted by Diego Velázquez can easily imagine her just a few years younger. The royal secretary's niece, our Queen's maid of honour, was fifteen years old and her beauty much more now than a mere promise. She had matured a great deal since the last time I had seen her: the laced bodice of her dress with its silver and coral edgings, matching the full brocade skirt held out stiffly around her hips by a farthingale, suggested curves that had not existed before. Ringlets of a purer gold than any Araucanian could have found in his mines still framed those blue eyes, complemented by her smooth white skin, which I imagined – and would one day find out for myself – had the same texture as silk.

'It's been a long time.'

She was so beautiful it was painful to look at her. The room with its Moorish columns overlooked a small garden in the palace, and the sun behind her created a white halo about her hair. Her smile was the same: mysterious and provocative with a hint of irony and mischief on her perfect lips.

'Yes, a long time,' I said at last.

The German had withdrawn to the garden, where I glimpsed the wimpled head of a duenna. Angélica sat down on a carved wooden chair and indicated that I should sit on the footstool in front of her. I did as she asked, not fully aware of what I was doing. She was studying me intently, her hands folded on her lap; from beneath the skirt of her dress emerged one slender satin slipper, and suddenly I was very conscious of my rough sleeveless doublet and darned shirt, my coarse trousers and military gaiters. *Oh, dear God*, I murmured to myself. I imagined the Court peacocks and fops of good blood and even better purses, dressed in all their finery, paying amorous compliments to Angélica at galas and gatherings. A jealous shiver pierced my soul.

'I hope,' she said very softly, 'that you bear me no malice.'

I remembered – and it took little effort – the humiliation, the prisons of the Inquisition in Toledo, the auto-da-fé in the Plaza Mayor and the role that Luis de Alquézar's niece had played in my misfortune. This thought had the virtue of restoring to me the coldness I so needed.

'What do you want from me?' I asked.

She took just a second longer than necessary to reply. She was still examining me closely, the same smile playing on her lips. She seemed pleased by what she saw.

'I don't want anything,' she said. 'I was simply

curious to see you again. I recognised you in the square.'

She fell silent for a moment. She looked at my hands and then again at my face.

'You've grown, sir.'

'So have you.'

She bit her lip slightly and nodded slowly. The ringlets gently brushed the pale skin of her cheeks, and I adored her.

'You've been fighting in Flanders.'

This was neither a statement nor a question. She appeared to be thinking aloud.

'I believe I love you,' she said suddenly.

I sprang to my feet. Angélica was no longer smiling. She was watching me from her chair, gazing up at me with eyes as blue as the sky, as the sea, as life itself. I swear she was lovely enough to drive a man insane.

'Great God,' I murmured.

I was trembling like the leaves on a tree. She remained motionless and silent for a long time. Finally she gave a slight shrug.

'I want you to know,' she said, 'that you have some very unfortunate friends – such as that Captain Batiste or Triste or whatever his name is – friends who are the enemies of my friends. And I want you to know that this could perhaps cost you your life.'

'It already nearly did,' I retorted.

'And it will do so again soon.'

Her smile had returned; it was the same smile as before, thoughtful and enigmatic.

'This evening,' she went on, 'the Duke and Duchess of Medina Sidonia are giving a party for the King and Queen. On the way back, my carriage will stop for a while in the Alameda. With its beautiful fountains and gardens, it's a delightful place to walk in.'

I frowned. This was all far too good and far too easy.

'Isn't that a little late for a walk.'

'We're in Seville. The nights are warm here.'

The irony of her words did not escape me. I glanced across at the courtyard, at the duenna still pacing up and down. Angélica understood my glance.

'She's not the same one who was with me at the Fuente del Acero . . . This one turns dumb and blind whenever I want her to. And I thought you might like to be at the Alameda tonight at ten, Íñigo Balboa.'

I stood there perplexed, analysing everything she had said.

'It's a trap,' I concluded, 'another ambush.'

'Possibly.' She held my gaze, her face inscrutable. 'It's up to you whether you're brave enough to fall into it or not.'

'The captain –' I began but stopped at once. Angélica stared at me with terrible perspicuity. It was as if she had read my thoughts.

'This captain fellow is your friend. You will doubtless have to tell him about this little secret . . . and no friend would allow you to walk alone into an ambush.'

She paused to allow the idea to penetrate.

'They say,' she added at last, 'that he too is a brave man.'

'Who says so?'

She did not reply, but merely smiled more broadly. And I understood then what she had just said to me. This certainty came with such astonishing clarity that I shuddered at the calculated way in which she was throwing this challenge in my face. Like a dark ghost, the black shape of Gualterio Malatesta interposed itself between us. It was all so obvious and so terrible: the old quarrel involved not only Alatriste now. I was of an age to answer for the consequences of my own actions; I knew too much, and as far as our enemies were concerned, I was as troublesome an adversary as the captain. Since I was the pretext for the rendezvous and since I had, perversely, been warned of the certain danger involved, I couldn't possibly go where Angélica was asking me to go, and yet I was incapable of not going. The words 'You've been fighting in Flanders' spoken only a moment before now took on a cruelly ironic tone. Ultimately, though, the message was intended for the captain, and I should not in that case keep it from him. However, if I told him, he would either forbid me to go to the Alameda or would forbid me to go alone. The letter of challenge was inevitably being issued to us both. It came down to a choice between my shame and certain danger. My conscience thrashed around like a fish caught in a net. Suddenly, Gualterio Malatesta's words surfaced in my memory with a sinister new meaning. Honour, he had said, is a dangerous thing to sustain.

'I wish to know,' said Angélica, 'if you are still prepared to die for me.'

I stared at her in bewilderment, incapable of saying a word. It was as if her gaze were walking freely around inside my mind.

'If you don't come,' she added, 'I will know that, despite your time spent in Flanders, you are a coward. If you do come, whatever happens, I want you to remember what I said before.'

The silk brocade of her dress rustled as she stood up. She was standing close to me now. Very close.

'And that I may well always love you.'

She looked across at the garden, where the duenna was walking up and down. Then she came still closer.

'Always remember that, to the very end . . . whenever that should come.'

'You're lying,' I said.

The blood suddenly seemed to have drained from my heart and my veins. Angélica continued studying me intently for what seemed an eternity. And then she did something unexpected, by which I mean that she raised one small white perfect hand and placed her fingers on my lips as softly as a kiss.

'Go,' she said.

She turned and went out into the garden. I was

so shaken that I took a few steps after her as if intending to follow her up to the royal apartments and into the Queen's private chambers. The German with the bushy side whiskers stopped me and, smiling, showed me to the door, at the same time returning my dagger.

I went and sat on the steps of the Casa Lonja, next to the cathedral, and stayed there for a long time, sunk in gloomy thoughts. I was filled with conflicting feelings, and my love for Angélica, revived by that disquieting interview, was locked in battle with the certain knowledge of the sinister trap closing around us. At first I considered saying nothing and making some excuse to slip away that night and go alone to the rendezvous, thus confronting my destiny with as my only companions my dagger and the constable's sword – a good blade made by the swordsmith Juanes which I kept wrapped in old rags, hidden in our room at the inn. But if I did that the venture was doomed. The shadowy figure of Malatesta took shape in my imagination like a dark omen. I would have no chance against him. And that of course was in the unlikely event that the Italian came to the rendezvous alone.

I felt like weeping with rage and impotence. I was a Basque and a hidalgo, the son of the soldier Lope Balboa, who had died in Flanders for the King and the true religion. My honour and the life of the man I respected most in the world hung in the balance, as did my life, but at that point in my existence – brought up as I had been from the age of twelve in the harsh worlds of criminality and war – I had already staked my life too often on the throw of a dice and possessed the fatalism of one who, with every breath, is aware how very easy it is to stop breathing altogether. I had seen too many men die – some uttering curses or weeping, some praying or silent, some despairing and others resigned – for dying to seem like anything extraordinary or terrible. Besides, I believed that there was another life beyond, where God, my own good father and all my old comrades would be waiting for me with open arms. And regardless of whether there was a life to come or not, I had learned that men like Captain Alatriste know that they can die at any moment, and death in the end always proves them right.

Such were my thoughts as I sat on the steps outside the Casa Lonja when in the distance I spotted the captain and the accountant Olmedilla. They were walking past the palace wall towards the Casa de Contratación. My first impulse was to run to meet them, but I stopped myself in time and instead merely observed the slender silent figure of my master, the broad brim of his hat shading his face, his sword bobbing at his side, and next to him the funereal presence of the accountant.

I watched them disappear round a corner then remained sitting motionless where I was, my arms around my knees. After all, I concluded, it was a simple enough matter. That night I merely had to decide between being killed alone or being killed alongside Captain Alatriste.

It was Olmedilla who proposed calling in at a tavern, and Diego Alatriste agreed, although the suggestion took him by surprise. This was the first time Olmedilla had ever proved talkative or sociable. They went towards the Seisdedos tavern, behind the building known as Las Atarazanas – the arsenal – and sat down at a table outside the door, underneath the porch and the awning that gave shelter from the sun. Alatriste removed his hat and placed it on a stool. A girl brought them a jug of Cazalla de la Sierra wine and a dish of purple olives, and Olmedilla drank with the captain. True, he barely tasted the wine, taking only a sip from his mug, but before doing so he took a long look at the man beside him. His brow unfurrowed slightly.

'Well played,' he said.

The captain studied the accountant's gaunt features, his sparse beard, his sallow parchment-like skin, which seemed to have been contaminated by the candles used to light gloomy government offices. He said nothing but simply raised the wine to his lips and, unlike Olmedilla, drained the mug to the lees. His companion continued to watch him with interest.

'They weren't exaggerating when they told me about you,' he said at last.

'That business with the Genoese fellow was easy,' replied Alatriste grimly and said no more, although the ensuing silence clearly stated: 'I've done other far more unsavoury things.' That at least is how Olmedilla appeared to interpret it, because he nodded slowly with the grave look of someone who understands and is too polite to ask further questions. As for Garaffa and his servant, they were at that moment sitting bound and gagged in a carriage that was driving them out of Seville to some destination unknown to the captain – he neither knew nor cared to know – with an escort of sinister-looking constables. Olmedilla had clearly alerted them beforehand, for they appeared in Calle del Mesón del Moro as if by magic – the neighbours' natural curiosity having been dampened by the fateful words 'Holy Office of the Inquisition' – then vanished discreetly with their prisoners in the direction of the Puerta de Carmona.

Olmedilla unbuttoned his doublet and took out a folded piece of paper bearing a seal. After holding it in his hand for a moment as if overcoming a few final scruples, he placed it on the table before the captain.

'It's an order of payment,' he said. 'To the bearer it's worth fifty old gold doubloons, double-headed . . . You can convert it into cash at the house of Don Joseph Arenzana, in Plaza de San Salvador. No questions asked.'

Alatriste looked at the piece of paper but did

not touch it. Double-headed doubloons were the most coveted coins of the day. They had been minted from fine gold over a century before, during the reign of the Catholic Kings, Fernando and Isabel, and no one doubted their value when you slammed them down on the table. He knew men who would knife their own mother for a single one of those doubloons.

'There'll be six times that amount,' added Olmedillo, 'when it's all over.'

'That's good to know.'

The accountant gazed thoughtfully into his wine. A fly was swimming about in it, making desperate attempts to clamber out.

'The fleet arrives in three days time,' he said, watching the dying fly.

'How many men will I need?'

Olmedilla pointed with an ink-stained finger at the order of payment.

'That's up to you. According to the Genoese fellow, the *Niklaasbergen* is carrying twenty or so sailors, a captain and a pilot, all of them apart from the pilot Flemish or Dutch. In Sanlúcar a few Spaniards might come on board with the cargo. And we only have one night.'

Alatriste made a rapid calculation.

'Twelve or fifteen then. With that amount of gold I can get all the men I need for the job.'

Olmedilla made a chary gesture with his hand, making it clear that Alatriste's 'job' was no business of his. He said: 'You should have them ready the night before. The plan is to go down the river and reach Sanlúcar by evening.' He sank his chin into his ruff, as if thinking hard to make sure he hadn't forgotten anything. 'I'll be coming too.'

'All the way?'

'We'll see.'

The captain made no attempt to conceal his surprise.

'It won't be a paper-and-ink affair.'

'That doesn't matter. Once the ship is in our hands, I have a duty to check the cargo and organise its transfer.'

Alatriste had to suppress a smile. He couldn't imagine the accountant mixing with the kind of people he was considering as recruits, but he could understand that in such matters one could never be too careful. So vast a quantity of gold was a temptation, and the odd ingot could easily get lost along the way.

'Needless to say,' added Olmedilla, 'any theft will be punishable by hanging.'

'Does that apply to you as well?'

'Perhaps, yes.'

Alatriste smoothed his moustache with one finger, then said drily, 'I shouldn't think they pay you enough for such alarming eventualities.'

'They pay sufficient for me to do my duty.'

The fly had ceased struggling, but Olmedilla continued to stare at it. The captain poured himself more wine. While he was drinking, he noticed that his companion had looked up again and was observing with some interest first the two scars on his forehead and then his left arm where his shirtsleeve concealed the burn beneath the bandage. The burn, by the way, stung like the very Devil. Finally Olmedilla frowned, as if he had been pondering a question he was afraid to ask.

'I was just wondering,' he said, 'what you would have done if Garaffa had been less easily intimidated.'

Alatriste glanced up and down the street, the dazzle of sun on the opposite wall making him half-close his eyes so that he appeared even more inscrutable. Then he looked at the drowned fly in Olmedilla's wine, took another sip from his own mug and said nothing.

CHAPTER 5

THE FIGHT

At the entrance to the Alameda the pillars of Hercules stood in the moonlight like two halberds. The tops of elm trees stretched out behind them as far as the eye could see, making the night seem still darker beneath the arbour of their branches. At that hour there were no carriages filled with elegant ladies and no Sevillean gentlemen on horse-back capering and caracoling amongst the bushes, fountains and pools. All I could hear was the sound of water and sometimes, in the distance, a dog barking anxiously somewhere near the chapel of La Cruz del Rodeo.

I stopped beside one of the thick stone pillars and listened, holding my breath. My throat was as dry as if it had been dusted with sand, and my pulse was pounding so hard in my wrists and temples that if at that moment someone had cut open my heart, they would have found not a drop of blood in it. As I fearfully scanned the Alameda, I pushed back my short cape to uncover the hilt of the sword I was wearing tucked in my leather belt. In such a deserted place the weight of the

113

sword, along with that of my dagger, was a great comfort to me. Then I checked the lacing on the buff coat that protected my torso. The coat belonged to Captain Alatriste, and I had 'borrowed' it from him while he was downstairs with Don Francisco de Quevedo and Sebastián Copons, eating and drinking and talking about Flanders. I had pretended to feel unwell and had retired early in order to carry out the plan that had been going round and round in my head all day. I gave my face and hair a thorough wash and then put on a clean shirt in case, at the end of the night, a scrap of that shirt should end up buried in my flesh. The captain's buff coat was rather too large for me, and so I had padded it out by wearing my old doublet underneath, stuffed with tow. I completed this outfit with a pair of much-patched chamois leather breeches that had survived the siege of Breda – and which would protect my thighs from any possible knife thrusts – a pair of buskins with esparto soles, some gaiters and a cap. Not exactly attire to go courting in, I thought when I saw my reflection in the copper bottom of a saucepan, but better a live ruffian than a dead fop.

I crept out with my buff coat and my sword concealed beneath my cape. Only Don Francisco spotted me briefly from afar, but he merely smiled and went on talking to the captain and Copons, who fortunately both had their backs to the door. Once in the street, I adjusted my clothing as best

114

I could as I walked towards the Plaza de San Francisco, and from there, avoiding the busier thoroughfares, I kept to Calle de las Sierpes and Calle del Puerco until I emerged into the deserted Alameda.

It was not, as it turned out, entirely deserted. A mule whinnied from beneath the elms. Frightened, I took a closer look, and when my eyes had grown accustomed to the gloom of that small wood, I could just make out the shape of a carriage standing next to one of the stone fountains. I moved forward cautiously, my hand resting on the hilt of my sword, until I could see the interior of the carriage, which was dimly lit by a covered lantern. Step by step, ever more slowly, I reached the running board.

'Good evening, soldier.'

That voice stole mine away and made the hand resting on my sword hilt tremble. Perhaps it wasn't a trap after all. Perhaps it was true that she loved me and was there, just as she had promised, waiting for me. I saw a male figure aloft on the driver's seat, and another at the rear: two silent servants watching over the Queen's maid of honour.

'I'm pleased to know you're not a coward,' whispered Angélica.

I took off my cap. In the dim glow of the lantern I could make out only vague shapes, but it was enough to light the upholstered interior, the golden glint of her hair and the satin of her dress when she shifted on her seat. I threw caution to the wind. The door was open, and I stepped up onto the running board. A delicious perfume wrapped about me like a caress. This, I thought, was the very perfume of her skin, and it was worth risking one's life for the mere bliss of being able to breathe it in.

'Have you come alone?'

'Yes.'

There was a long silence. When she spoke again, she sounded surprised.

'You're very stupid,' she said, 'and very noble.'

I did not respond. I was too happy to spoil the moment with words. In the half-dark I could see her eyes shining. She was still looking at me without saying a word. I touched the satin of her skirt and finally managed to murmur, 'You said you loved me.'

There was an even longer silence, interrupted by the impatient whinnying of the mules. I heard the driver quieten them with a flick of the reins. The servant at the back was still only a dark motionless smudge.

'Did I?' She paused, as if struggling to remember what it was we had talked about that morning at the palace. 'Perhaps I do,' she concluded.

'I love you,' I declared.

'Is that why you're here?'

'Yes.'

She bent her face towards mine. I swear I felt her hair brush my cheek.

'In that case,' she whispered, 'you deserve a reward.'

She placed one hand on my face with infinite tenderness, and suddenly I felt her lips pressed to mine. For a moment they remained there, soft and cool. Then she withdrew into the carriage.

'That is just an advance payment on my debt to you,' she said. 'If you survive, you can claim the rest.'

She gave an order to the coachman, and he cracked his whip. The carriage moved off. I stood there dumbstruck, clutching my cap in one hand and with the fingers of my other hand incredulously touching the mouth that Angélica de Alquézar had just kissed. The universe was spinning, and it took me a while to recover my sanity.

Then I looked about me and saw the shadows.

They were emerging out of the darkness, from amongst the trees. Seven dark shapes, men with faces obscured by cloaks and hats. They approached slowly, as if they had all the time in the world, and beneath my buff coat I could feel my skin prickle.

'Damnation!' said a voice. 'It's the boy and he's come alone!'

This time there was no *tiruri-ta-ta*, but I immediately recognised the harsh, hoarse, cracked tone. It came from the shadow nearest to me, which seemed very tall and black. They were standing round me, not moving, as if uncertain what to do with me.

'Such a very big net,' added the voice, 'to catch one sardine.'

The scorn with which this was said had the virtue of heating my blood and restoring my composure. The panic that had begun to fill me vanished. Those faceless men might not know what to do with the sardine, but the sardine had spent all day deliberating and preparing himself for precisely this situation. Every outcome, even the very worst, had been weighed and pondered and considered a hundred times in my imagination, and I was ready. My only regret was that I had no time to perform a proper act of contrition, but there was nothing to be done about it. And so I undid my cape, took a deep breath, made the sign of the cross and unsheathed my sword. What a shame, I thought, that Captain Alatriste could not see me now. He would have been pleased to know that the son of his friend Lope Balboa also knew how to die.

'Well, well—' said Malatesta.

Sheer surprise meant that his comment remained unfinished as I adopted a proper fencing stance and made a lunge that went straight through his cloak, missing his body by an inch. He stepped back to avoid me, and I still had time to deliver a back-edged cut before he had even put hand to sword. That sword, however, now left its sheath with a sinister whisper, and I saw the blade glitter as the Italian moved away to take off his cape and assume the on-guard position.

Feeling that my one opportunity was slipping away, I steadied myself and closed on him again, and despite my fear remained in control, abruptly raising my arm to make a feint to his head, then changing sides and, with the same back-edged cut, I lunged forward as I had before, with such verve that, if my enemy had not been wearing a hat, his soul would have been sent straight down to Hell.

Gualterio Malatesta stumbled back, blaspheming loudly in Italian. And then, convinced that any initial advantage I might have had ended there, I swung round, describing a circle with the point of my sword, to confront the others who, also taken by surprise, had finally unsheathed their weapons and surrounded me with no consideration for my solitary state. The sentence was clear, as clear as the light of day that I would never see again. The rapid thought crossed my mind that for a boy from Oñate this wasn't such a bad way to end, and, taking my dagger in my left hand, I prepared to defend myself. One against seven.

'Leave him to me,' Malatesta said to his companions.

He had recovered from his initial shock and came towards me confidently, sword at the ready, and I knew that I had only a few more seconds of life left. And so instead of waiting for him in the on-guard stance, as prescribed in the true art of swordplay, I half-crouched down, then sprang up like a hare and aimed straight at his chest. My blade, however, pierced only air. Inexplicably Malatesta was now behind me, and I could feel his knife pressing into one shoulder in the gap between buff coat and shirt from which protruded the tow from the doublet I was wearing underneath.

'You're going to die like a man, boy,' said Malatesta.

There was both anger and admiration in his voice, but I had passed that point of no return where words are of interest, and I didn't give a fig for his admiration, his anger or his scorn. And so without a word I turned, as I had so often seen Captain Alatriste do: knees bent, dagger in one hand and sword in the other, reserving my breath for the final attack. I had once heard the captain say that the thing that helps a man to die well is knowing that he has done all he can to avoid death.

Then from the encircling gloom came a pistol shot, and my enemies were briefly lit up by the glare. One of them had not yet hit the ground when the Alameda was lit by another flash, and in that burst of light I saw Captain Alatriste, Copons and Don Francisco de Quevedo rushing towards us, swords in hand, as if they had sprung from the bowels of the earth.

Thank God they came when they did. The night became a storm of knives, clanging steel, sparks and shouts. There were two bodies on the ground and eight men fighting – a confusion of shadows that could only occasionally be recognised by their voices – all furiously fencing, shoving and stumbling. I took my sword in my hand and went straight over to the man nearest to me and, in the melee, and with an ease that surprised me, I stuck a good quarter of my blade into his back. I drove it in and pulled it out, and, with a howl, the wounded man spun round – which is how I knew it was not Malatesta – and made a ferocious lunge at me which I managed to parry with my dagger, although he broke its guard, bruising the fingers of my left hand. I hurled myself at him, drawing back my arm, swordpoint foremost. I felt his knife graze my buff coat, but I did not jump back; instead, I trapped the blade between my elbow and my side and meanwhile ran him through again, plunging my sword right in this time, so that we both fell to the ground. I raised my dagger to finish him off right there and then, but he was no longer moving and from his throat came the hoarse stertorous rattle of someone drowning in his own blood. I placed my knee on his chest so as to remove my sword and then returned to the fray.

Things were more even-handed now. Copons, whom I could identify by his short stature, was locked in combat with an opponent who, between blows, kept uttering the most terrible oaths, until suddenly his curses were replaced by groans. Don Francisco de Quevedo was limping back and forth between two adversaries – both far less skilled than he – and fighting with his usual panache. Meanwhile, Captain Alatriste, who had sought out Malatesta in the midst of the skirmish, was doing battle with him a little way off, next to one of the stone fountains. They and their swords stood out against the shimmer of moonlight on water, as they lunged and drew back, performing feints, body feints and terrifying thrusts. I noticed that the Italian had abandoned both his loquacity and his wretched whistling. It was not a night to waste one's breath on fripperies.

A shadow came between me and them. My arm was aching now from so much movement, and I was beginning to feel tired. Lunges and slices began to rain down on me, and I retreated, covering myself as best I could, which I did quite successfully. I was afraid I might fall into one of the ponds which I knew were somewhere behind me, although of course a soaking is always preferable to a stabbing. I was rescued from this dilemma by Sebastián Copons, who, having rid himself of his adversary, now confronted mine, forcing him to deal with attacks from two fronts. Copons fought like a machine, closing on the other man and forcing him to pay more attention to him than to me. I decided to slip round to his side and knife the man as soon as Copons got in his next blow, and was just about to do so when, from the direction of the Hospital del Amor de Dios beyond the stone pillars, came lights and voices crying, 'Halt!' and 'Stop in the name of the King's justice!'

'The bluebottles are here!' muttered Quevedo in between thrusts.

The first to take to his heels was the man under

122

attack by Copons and myself, and, before you could say knife, Don Francisco found himself alone as well. Of our opponents, three lay on the ground and a fourth was crawling away into the bushes moaning. We went over to join the captain and, when we reached the fountain, found him sword in hand staring into the shadows into which Gualterio Malatesta had disappeared.

'Let's go,' said Quevedo.

The lights and voices of the constables were getting closer. They were still calling out in the name of the King and of justice, but they were in no hurry to arrive, fearful of the situation they might find themselves in.

'What about Íñigo?' asked the captain, still gazing after his vanished enemy.

'Íñigo's fine.'

That was when Alatriste turned to look at me. In the faint glow of moonlight I thought I could see his eyes fixed on me.

'Never do that again,' he said.

I swore that I never would. Then we picked up our hats and cloaks and ran off into the shadows under the elm trees.

Many years have passed since then. Now, whenever I go back to Seville, I visit the Alameda – which has barely changed since I first saw it – and there, time and again, I let my mind fill up with memories. There are certain places that mark the geography of a man's life, and that was one of them, as was the Portillo de las Ánimas, as were the dungeons of Toledo, the plains of Breda and the fields of Rocroi. The Alameda de Hércules however occupies a special place. During my time in Flanders I had, without noticing it, matured, but I only knew this for certain on that night in Seville when I found myself alone, face to face with the Italian and his henchmen and wielding a sword. Angélica de Alquézar and Gualterio Malatesta had unwittingly done me the great favour of making me realise this fact. And thus I learned that it is easy to fight when your comrades are near or when the woman you love is watching you, giving you vigour and courage. The hard thing is to fight alone in the dark, with no other witnesses but your honour and your conscience. With no reward and no hope.

By God, it's been a long road. All the people in this story – the captain, Quevedo, Gualterio Malatesta, Angélica de Alquézar – died a long time ago, and only in these pages can I make them live again and recapture them exactly as they were. Their ghosts – some loved, some loathed – remain intact in my memory, along with that harsh violent fascinating time which for me will always be the Spain of my youth and the Spain of Captain Alatriste. Now my hair is grey, and my memories are as bittersweet as all clear-sighted memories are, and I share the same weariness with which they all seemed to be burdened. With the passing years I have learned that one pays for clear-sightedness with despair, and that the life we Spaniards lead has always been a slow road to nowhere. While travelling my section of that road I have lost many things and gained a few more. Now, on this apparently interminable journey – it even occurs to me sometimes that perhaps I, Íñigo Balboa, will never die – I can at least enjoy the resignation of memories and silence. And now, at last, I understand why all the heroes I admired back then were so very weary.

I hardly slept that night. Lying on my mattress, I could hear the captain's steady breathing while I watched the moon slip behind one corner of the open window. My head was as hot as if I were suffering from the ague and my sheets were drenched in sweat. From the nearby bawdy house came the occasional sound of a woman laughing or the chords of a guitar.

Feverish and unable to sleep, I left my bed, went over to the window in my bare feet and leaned on the sill. In the moonlight the rooftops looked unreal and the clothes hung out to dry on the flat roofs resembled white shrouds. I was of course thinking about Angélica.

I didn't hear Captain Alatriste until he was by my side. He was wearing only his nightshirt and, like me, was barefoot. He too stood gazing into the darkness, saying nothing, and out of the corner of my eye I could see his aquiline nose, his pale eyes absorbed in the strange light from outside and the bushy moustache that only emphasised his formidable soldier's profile.

'She is loyal to her own,' he said at last.

That 'she' in his mouth made me tremble. I nodded, still without saying a word. I was at an age when I would have argued with anything else he might have had to say on the subject but not with that unexpected comment. It was something I could understand.

'It's only natural,' he added.

I didn't know whether he was referring to Angélica or to my own warring emotions. Suddenly a feeling of unease rose up inside me, a strange sadness.

'I love her,' I murmured.

No sooner had I spoken these words than I felt intensely ashamed, but the captain did not make fun of me nor did he offer any trite words of advice. He simply stood there not moving, contemplating the night.

'We all love once,' he said. 'Or, indeed, several times.'

'Several times?'

My question seemed to catch him off guard. He paused for a moment, as if he thought it his duty to say something more but he didn't quite know what. He cleared his throat. I noticed him shifting uncomfortably.

'One day it stops,' he said at last. 'That's all.'

'I'll always love her.'

The captain hesitated before responding.

'Of course,' he said. He remained silent for a moment, then said again very softly, 'Of course.'

126

I felt him raising one hand to place it on my shoulder, just as he had in Flanders on the day that Sebastián Copons slit the throat of that wounded Dutchman after the battle at Ruyter mill. This time, however, he did not complete his gesture.

'Your father . . .'

Again, he left the words hanging inconclusively in the air. Perhaps, I thought, he wanted to tell me that his friend Lope Balboa would have been proud to see me that night, sword and dagger in hand, alone against seven men and only sixteen years old. Or to hear his son saying that he was in love with a woman.

'You did very well in the Alameda just now.'

I blushed with pride. In Captain Alatriste's mouth these words were worth a Genoese banker's ransom. It was the equivalent of a king commanding a subject to don his hat in his presence.

'I knew it was a trap,' I said.

The last thing I wanted was for him to think that I had fallen into the trap like some novice. The captain nodded reassuringly.

'I know you did. And I know that it wasn't intended for you.'

'Angélica de Alquézar,' I said as steadily as I could, 'is entirely my affair.'

Now he remained silent for a long time. I was staring obstinately out of the window and the captain was watching me.

'Of course,' he said again at last.

The scenes of that day kept crowding into my mind. I touched my mouth where she had placed her lips. 'If you survive,' she had said, 'you can claim the rest.' I turned pale at the thought of those seven shadows emerging out of the darkness beneath the trees. My shoulder still hurt from the knife thrust stopped by the Captain's buff coat and my tow-stuffed doublet.

'One day,' I muttered, almost thinking out loud, 'I'll kill Gualterio Malatesta.'

I heard the captain chuckle. There was no mockery in that laughter, no scorn for my young man's arrogance. It was a gentle laugh, warm and affectionate.

'Possibly,' he said, 'but first I must have a go at killing him myself.'

The next day we planted our imaginary flag and started recruiting. We did so as discreetly as possible, with no ensigns, no drum roll and no sergeants. And Seville was the ideal place to provide the kind of men we required. When you think about it, man's first father was a thief, his first mother a liar and their first son a murderer – for there's nothing new under the sun – and this family history of crime was confirmed in that rich and turbulent city where the Ten Commandments weren't so much broken as hacked to pieces with a knife. Seville, with its taverns, bawdy houses and gaming dens, with the Corral de Los Naranjos and even the royal prison – which quite rightly bore the title of the Spanish empire's capital of crime – abounded in purveyors of stranglings and dealers in sword thrusts; and this was only natural in a city populated by gentlemen of fortune, hidalgos of thievery, caballeros who appeared to live on air and with not a thought for the morrow, and monks of the Holy Order of Intrigue, a city where judges and constables could be silenced with a gag of silver. It was, in short, a university for the biggest rogues God ever created, full of churches offering sanctuary, and a place where men would kill on credit for a *maravedi*, a woman or a word.

> *Remember Gonzalo Xeniz,*
> *Gayoso and Ahumada,*
> *Those butchers of bodies*
> *And scarrers of faces . . .*

The problem was that in a city like Seville, indeed in the whole of Spain, where all was bravado and effrontery, many of these self-proclaimed killers were nothing but talk, young ruffians full of valiant oaths who in their cups claimed to have dispatched between twenty and thirty men, boasting of murders they hadn't committed and of wars in which they hadn't served, of how they were as happy to kill with their bare hands as with a knife or a sword, strutting and swaggering in buff coats and hats as large as parasols, and sporting black looks, goatee beards and moustaches that resembled the guard on a dagger. However, come the moment of truth, twenty of them together wouldn't have been capable of seeing off one drunk constable, and if tortured on the rack they would have confessed everything at the first turn of the screw. If you were not to be dazzled by such an apparent abundance of fine swordsmen, you had to know who you were dealing with, as Captain Alatriste most certainly did. Thus, relying on the captain's keen eye, we began our levy in the taverns of La Heria and Triana, in search of old acquaintances who were men of few words but had a ready hand with the sword, who were not stage villains but genuine ruffians, men who would kill without giving their victims time to confess, so that no one afterwards could go telling tales to the law. The kind of man who, when questioned under pain of death, and when the torturer turned the screw, would offer as guarantors only his own throat and spine, and remain entirely dumb except to say nought or my name's Nobody or to call on the Church itself for aid, but otherwise offer no information, not even if someone promised to dub him a Knight of Calatrava.

Alonso Fierro, fencing master
Skilled with sword and dagger,
Slit many a throat in old Seville,
One doubloon per funeral.

Calling on the Church wasn't, in fact, such a bad idea, for Seville boasted the most famous refuge for rogues in the world, the cathedral's Corral de los Naranjos, whose renown and usefulness is captured in these lines:

I ran away from Córdoba
And reached Seville a tired man.
There I became a gardener
In the Corral de los Naranjos.

This was one of the courtyards in the cathedral or Iglesia Mayor, which had been built on the site of the former Moorish mosque, just as the Giralda tower had been modelled on a minaret. It was a pleasant spacious area with a fountain in the middle and was shaded by the orange trees from which it took its name. The main door from this famous courtyard opened onto the cathedral square and the surrounding steps, which during the day, like the steps of San Felipe in Madrid, were the favoured place for idlers and rogues to meet and talk. Because of the courtyard's role as a sanctuary, it became the chosen place of asylum for desperados, scoundrels and criminals on the run from justice, and there they lived freely and well, visited both day and night by their whores and companions; and these men whom the law was most eager to apprehend only ventured forth into the city in large gangs, so that even the constables themselves dared not confront them. The place has been described by the sharpest quills of Spanish letters, from the great Don Miguel de Cervantes to Don Francisco de Quevedo, so I need not provide much detail here. No picaresque novel, no soldier's tale or rogue's story is complete without a mention of Seville and the Corral de lost Naranjos. Simply try to imagine the atmosphere of that legendary place, close by the Casa Lonja and the shops selling silk, a place where fugitives from justice and the whole criminal world were as thick as thieves, as snug as bugs in a rug.

I accompanied the captain on his recruiting campaign, and we visited the Corral during the day, when the light was still good and it was easy to recognise faces. On the steps up to the main entrance beat the pulse of that multifarious and sometimes cruel city of Seville. At that hour the steps were seething with idlers, sellers of cheap trinkets, strollers, rogues, streetwalkers with their faces half-veiled, young female pickpockets disguised as innocent maids accompanied by ancient chaperones and little pages, with light-fingered thieves, beggars and blades for hire. In the midst of them all a blind man was selling ballad sheets and singing about the death of Escamilla:

> 'Brave, bold Escamilla,
> Glory and pride of all Sevilla . . .'

Half a dozen ruffians were gathered beneath the arch of the main doorway and nodded approvingly as they listened to the turbulent story of that legendary swordsman and hired assassin, the very cream of the local villainry. We passed them as we went into the courtyard, and I couldn't help noticing that the whole group turned to watch Captain Alatriste. Inside, thirty or so fellows identical in appearance to those at the entrance were lounging in the shade of the orange trees next to the pleasant fountain. In this market of death contracts to kill were regularly drawn up and agreed. This was the refuge for the kind of men who would slice open a face or relieve a soul of its corruptible matter. They had more steel about their persons than a Toledo sword-smith, and they all sported Córdoba leather jerkins, turned-down boots, broad-brimmed hats, large moustaches and a swaggering, bow-legged gait. Otherwise, the Corral resembled a gypsy encampment, with pots being heated over fires, blankets spread on the ground, bundles of clothing, a few mats on which men were dozing and a couple of gaming tables, one for cards and the other for dice, where a jug of wine was doing the rounds amongst gamblers intent on wagering their very souls, even though the latter had been in hock to the Devil ever since their owners were weaned. A few ruffians were in close conversation with their women, some of whom were young and others less so, but who all conformed to the same whorish pattern, hard-faced and hardworking, accounting to their pimps for the money they earned on the street corners of Seville.

Alatriste stopped by the fountain and quickly

looked around. I was right behind him, fascinated by everything I saw. One bold doxy, her cloak folded and draped across her chest as if she were ready for a knife fight, casually and brazenly accosted him. When they heard her do this, two cut-throats playing dice at one of the tables got up very slowly, giving us a mean appraising look. They were dressed in typical ruffian style – open-necked shirts with wide Walloon collars, coloured hose and baldrics about a span wide – and were equipped with all kinds of swords and daggers. The younger of the two was carrying on his belt a pistol instead of a dagger and held a light cork shield.

'What can we do for you, sir?' asked one.

The captain turned to them calmly, his thumbs in his belt, his hat down over his eyes.

'Nothing, gentlemen,' he said. 'I'm looking for a friend.'

'Perhaps we know him,' said the other man.

'Perhaps,' replied the captain, again looking around.

The two fellows exchanged a glance. A third man who had been watching came over, curious to know what was going on. I shot a sideways look at the captain and saw that he was entirely unruffled. After all this was his world too, and he knew it like the back of his hand.

'You probably want—' began one.

Alatriste ignored him and walked on. I went behind, keeping my eye on the two cut-throats, who were discussing in low voices whether the captain's behaviour constituted an affront and if so whether or not they should knife him in the back. They were clearly unable to reach agreement, for nothing happened. The captain was now studying a group sitting in the shade by a wall – three men and two women apparently engaged in animated conversation as they swigged from a capacious leather wineskin. Then I saw that he was smiling.

He went over to the group, and I followed. When they saw us approaching, the conversation gradually petered out, and the various members of the group eyed us warily. One of the men had very dark skin and hair and huge side whiskers that reached right down to his jaw. He had a couple of marks on his face which had clearly not been there since birth and large blunt-nailed hands. He was dressed almost entirely in leather, had a short broad Toledo sword – the blade of which bore its maker's unusual mark: an engraving of a puppy – and his coarse canvas breeches were adorned with strange green and yellow bows. He sat staring at my master as the latter came towards him, and his words died on his lips.

'Well, I'll be hanged,' he said at last, open-mouthed, 'if it isn't Captain Alatriste.'

'The only thing that surprises me, Señor Don Juan Jaqueta, is that they haven't hanged you already.'

The man uttered a couple of oaths and a loud guffaw and then stood up brushing off his breeches.

'So where have you sprung from?' he asked, shaking the captain's proffered hand.

'Here and there.'

'Are you in hiding too?'

'No, just visiting.'

'By my faith, I'm pleased to see you!'

Jaqueta cheerily demanded the wineskin from his companions; this was duly passed round, and even I drank my share. After exchanging memories of mutual friends and of the odd shared experience – which is how I learned that Jaqueta had also been in Naples as a soldier, and was one of the best too, and that, years before, Alatriste himself had taken refuge in that very place – Jaqueta, my master and I moved away from the group. The captain came straight to the point and told Jaqueta that he had some work for him, his kind of work with a promise of gold paid in advance.

'Here?'

'In Sanlúcar.'

Jaqueta made a despairing gesture.

'If it were something easy and a night job,' he explained, 'that would be fine. But I can't stray very far at the moment. A week ago I knifed a merchant, the brother-in-law of a cathedral canon, and the law's after me.'

'That can be sorted out.'

Jaqueta gave my master a keen look.

'Blind me, do you have a letter from the Archbishop or something?'

'Better than that,' said the captain, patting his doublet. 'I have a document authorising me to recruit whatever friends I can and to place them beyond the reach of the law.'

'Are you serious?'

'I certainly am.'

'Things are obviously going well for you.' Jaqueta spoke more respectfully now. 'I imagine the job will involve some, shall we say, hand work.'

'You imagine correctly.'

'Just you and me?'

'Plus a few others.'

Jaqueta was scratching his side whiskers. He glanced over at his companions and lowered his voice.

'And there's cash aplenty, is there?'

'There is.'

'Part payment in advance?'

'Three double-headed doubloons.'

Jaqueta let out an admiring whistle.

'Well, I could certainly do with that; the wages for our kind of work have gone right down, Captain. Only yesterday someone came to see me about doing away with his good lady's lover and all he was offering was twenty ducados. What do you think to that?'

'Shameful.'

'Too true,' agreed Jaqueta, his fist on his hip, every inch the ruffian now. 'So I told him that all he could get for that price was a cut to the face that would require ten stitches, twelve at most. We argued, got nowhere, and I very nearly knifed him there and then, and I'd have done it for free too.'

Alatriste was once more looking around him.

'I need men I can trust, good swordsmen, not playhouse villains. And I want no telltales either.'

Jaqueta nodded authoritatively.

'How many?'

'A good dozen.'

'It's a big job then.'

'You don't think I'd be looking for such a rabble just to knife an old lady, do you?'

'No, of course not. Is it dangerous work?'

'Fairly.'

Jaqueta frowned thoughtfully.

'Most of the men here are pure scum,' he said, 'no good for anything but cutting the ears off cripples or giving their whores a good belting when they bring back four *reales* less than they should after a day's work.' He discreetly indicated one man in his group. 'He might be all right. His name's Sangonera and he's been a soldier too. A nasty piece of work, but good with his hands and fast on his feet. And I know a mulatto who's hiding out at San Salvador church at the moment. His name's Campuzano. He's as strong as an ox and knows how to hold his tongue – why, only six months ago they tried to pin a murder on him, which he and another lad had in fact done, but he survived four bouts of strappado like a pure-bred hidalgo because he knows that you pay for any slip of the tongue with your throat.'

'Sensible man,' commented Alatriste.

'After all,' went on Jaqueta philosophically, 'it takes no more effort to say a no than a yes, does it?'

'Very true.'

Alatriste looked at the man called Sangonera, who was sitting with the rest of the group by the wall. He was thinking.

'Sangonera it is, then,' he said at last, 'if you can vouch for him and if I still like him when we've spoken. I'll take a look at that mulatto too, but I still need more people.'

Jaqueta wore an expression of deep concentration.

'There are some other good comrades in Seville at the moment, like Ginesillo el Lindo or Guzmán Ramírez – both men with blood in their veins. You remember Ginesillo, I'm sure. He once killed a catchpole for calling him a shirtlifter. Oh, it must be ten, fifteen years ago now, around the time you were living here in Seville.'

'Yes, I remember Ginesillo,' said Alatriste.

'Well, you'll also remember that they tortured him by holding his head under water. Three times they did it, and he didn't so much as blink, far less squeal on anyone.'

'I'm surprised they didn't burn him at the stake. They usually do with his sort.'

Jaqueta burst out laughing.

'He's not only turned mute, he's got very dangerous indeed, and there's not a catchpole brave enough to lay a hand on him. I don't know where he lives, but he's sure to be at the royal prison tonight for Nicasio Ganzúa's wake.'

139

'Who's Ganzúa? I don't know him.'

Jaqueta quickly told Alatriste all about Ganzúa, one of the most celebrated ruffians in Seville, the terror of catchpoles and the pride of Seville's taverns, gaming dens and bawdy houses. He had been walking along a narrow street one day when the Count of Niebla's carriage spattered him with mud. The Count was with his servants and a few young friends of his; there was an exchange of words, swords were drawn, Ganzúa dispatched one of the servants and one of the friends, but by some miracle the Count himself escaped with only a stab wound to the thigh. A regiment of constables and catchpoles came after Ganzúa, and at the hearing even though he didn't say a word someone mentioned a few other little matters pending, including a couple of murders and a notorious jewel robbery carried out in Calle Platería. In short, Ganzúa was to be garrotted the next day in Plaza de San Francisco.

'A shame really, because he would have been perfect for what we have in mind,' said Jaqueta regretfully, 'but there's no getting him out of tomorrow's execution. Tonight, though, his comrades will join him for a final meal and help him on his way, you know, the usual thing. Ginesillo and Ramírez are good friends of his, so you'll probably find them there.'

'I'll go to the prison then,' said Alatriste.

'Well, say hello to Ganzúa from me. A man needs his friends at times like this, and I'd be there like

140

a shot if I could.' Jaqueta examined me closely. 'Who's the boy?'

'A friend.'

'Bit green, isn't he?' Jaqueta continued to study me inquisitively and noticed the dagger in my belt. 'Is he involved in this?'

'On and off.'

'That's a nice weapon he's carrying.'

'And he knows how to use it too.'

'Well, we ruffians have to start young, don't we?'

The conversation moved on, and everything was agreed for the next day, with Alatriste promising to alert the law officers so that Jaqueta could leave the Corral in safety. We said our goodbyes and spent the rest of the day on our recruitment campaign, which took us first to La Heria and Triana, and then to San Salvador, where the mulatto Campuzano – a giant black man with a sword like a scimitar – also proved to the captain's liking. By evening my master had signed up half a dozen men to his company: Jaqueta, Sangonera, the mulatto, an extremely hirsute Murcian called Pencho Bullas – highly thought of by the other rogues – and two former soldiers from the galleys known as Enríquez el Zurdo, 'Enriquez the Left-hander', and Andresito el de los Cincuenta, the latter having earned his nickname from the time when he had received fifty lashes and taken them like a man. A week later the sergeant who had ordered the flogging was found lying near the Puerta de la Carne with his throat neatly cut, and no one could ever prove – although they could easily imagine – who had done the job.

We still needed more pairs of hands, and in order to complete our singular and well-armed company Diego Alatriste decided to go to the royal prison that night and attend the ruffian Ganzúa's final meal. But I will tell you about that in more detail, for Seville's prison, I can assure you, deserves a chapter to itself.

CHAPTER 6

THE ROYAL PRISON

That night we attended Nicasio Ganzúa's last meal, but first I spent some time on a personal matter that was troubling me greatly. And although I learned nothing new from the exercise, it served at least to distract me from the unease I was feeling about Angélica de Alquézar's role in what had happened in the Alameda. My steps thus led me once more to the palace – where I patrolled the entire length of its walls – as well as to the Arco de la Judería and the palace gate, where I stood watching for a while amongst the onlookers. This time, the soldiers guarding the palace were not the ones in red and yellow uniforms, but Burgundy archers dressed in their striking red-chequered garb and carrying short pikes, and I was relieved not to see the fat sergeant, which meant that there would be no repeat of our earlier confrontation. The square opposite the palace was teeming with people, for the King and Queen were going to the cathedral to pray a solemn rosary, after which they would receive a delegation from the city of Jerez. There was more to the latter engagement than met the

143

eye, and it might be worth explaining that at the time Jerez, like Galicia before it, was hoping to buy representation at the Cortes de la Corona, the Cortes of the King, in order to escape its current subjection to the influence of Seville. In that Habsburg Spain-cum-marketplace there was nothing unusual about buying a seat at the Cortes – the city of Palencia was trying to do the same thing – and the amount offered by the men from Jerez came to the respectable sum of 85,000 ducats, all of which would of course end up in the King's coffers. The deal foundered, however, when Seville counter-attacked by bribing the Council of the Treasury, and the final judgement made was that the request would only be granted on condition that the money came not from contributions made by the citizens but from the private wealth of the twenty-four municipal magistrates who wanted the seat. The prospect of having to dip into their own pockets put a completely different perspective on the matter, and the Jerez corporation withdrew the request. This all helps to explain the role that the Cortes played at the time, as well as the submissive attitude of the Cortes of Castile and of others, for – rights and privileges apart – these other Cortes were only listened to when their votes were needed for new taxes or for subsidies to replenish the royal treasury, or to pay for wars or the general expenses of a monarchy that the Count-Duke of Olivares deemed to be a powerful and unifying force. Unlike in France and England, where the kings had destroyed the power of the feudal lords and agreed terms with the merchants and traders – for neither that red-haired whore Elizabeth I nor that vile Frenchy Richelieu were ever ones for half-measures – in Spain the noble and the powerful formed two groups: those who obeyed royal authority meekly and almost abjectly (by and large ruined Castilians who had no other protection than that of the King) and those on the periphery, cushioned by local charters and ancient privileges, who protested loudly whenever called upon to defray costs or equip armies. The Church, of course, did exactly as it chose. Most political activity, therefore, consisted of a constant to and fro of haggling, usually over money; and all the subsequent crises that we endured under Philip IV – the Medina Sidonia plot in Andalusia, the Duke of Híjar's conspiracy in Aragon, the secession of Portugal and the Catalonia War – were created by two things: the royal treasury's greed and a reluctance on the part of the nobility, the clerics and large local merchants to pay anything at all. The sole object of the King's visit to Seville both in 1624 and now was to crush local opposition to a vote in favour of new taxes. The sole obsession of that unhappy Spain was money, which is why the route to the Indies was so crucial. To demonstrate how little this had to do with justice or decency, suffice it to say that two or three years earlier the Cortes had rejected outright a luxury tax to be levied on sinecures, gratuities, pensions and rents, that is to say, on the rich. The Venetian ambassador Contarini was alas quite right when he wrote at the time, 'The most effective war one can wage on the Spanish is to leave them to be devoured and destroyed by their own bad governance.'

But let us return to my own troubles. As I was saying, I spent the whole afternoon in the vicinity of the palace and in the end my determination was rewarded, albeit only in part, for the gates finally opened, the Burgundy archers formed a guard of honour, and the King and Queen accompanied by the nobility and the authorities of Seville walked the short distance to the cathedral. The young and very beautiful Queen Isabel nodded graciously to the crowd. Sometimes she smiled with that peculiarly French charm which did not always quite fit in with the rigid etiquette of the Spanish Court. She was carrying a gold rosary and a small prayer book decorated with mother-of-pearl, and was dressed according to the Spanish fashion in a gold-embroidered costume of blue satin with sleeves slashed to reveal an underlayer of silver cloth, and, draped over her head and shoulders, an exquisite white lace mantilla sewn with pearls. Arm in arm with her walked the equally youthful King, Philip IV, as fair, pale, stern-faced and inscrutable as ever. He was wearing a costume made of silver-grey velvet with a neat Walloon collar, a gold Agnus Dei medallion studded with diamonds, a golden sword and

146

a hat topped with white feathers. The Queen's pleasant demeanour and friendly smile stood in marked contrast to her august husband's solemn presence, for he still conformed to the grave Burgundian model of behaviour brought from Flanders by the Emperor Charles which meant that – apart from when he was actually walking of course – he never moved foot, hand or head, but always kept his gaze directed upward as if the only person he had to justify himself to was God. No one, either in public or in private, had ever seen him lose his perfect composure and no one ever would. On that afternoon I would never have dreamed that life would later present me with the opportunity to serve and escort the King at a very difficult time for both him and Spain, and I can state categorically that he always maintained that same imperturbable – and ultimately legendary – sangfroid. Not that he was disagreeable; he was extremely fond of poetry, plays and other literary diversions, of the arts and of gentlemanly pursuits. Nor did he lack personal courage, although he never set foot on a battlefield except from afar and years later, during the war with Catalonia. However, when it came to his great passion, hunting, he often ran real risks and even killed wild boar on his own. He was a consummate horseman, and once, as I have recounted before, he won the admiration of the people by dispatching a bull in the Plaza Mayor in Madrid with a single shot from a harquebus. His failings

147

were a certain weakness of character that led him to leave the business of the monarchy entirely in the hands of the Count-Duke and his unbounded liking for women, which once – as I will describe on another occasion – very nearly cost him his life. Otherwise, he never had the grandeur or the energy of his great-grandfather the Emperor, or the tenacious intelligence of his grandfather Philip II. But although he devoted far too much time to his own amusements, indifferent to the clamour of a hungry population, to the anger of ill-governed territories and kingdoms, to the fragmentation of the empire he had inherited, and to Spain's military and maritime ruin, it is fair to say that his kindly nature never provoked any feelings of personal hostility, and right up until his death he was loved by the people, who attributed most of the country's misfortunes to his favourites, his ministers and advisers, in a Spain that was at the time far too large, beleaguered by far too many enemies, and so in thrall to base human nature that not even the risen Christ would have been capable of preserving it intact.

In the cortège I spotted the Count-Duke of Olivares, as imposing a figure as ever, both physically and in the way his every gesture and look exuded absolute power; also present was the elegant young son of the Duke of Medina Sidonia, the Count of Niebla, who was accompanying Their Majesties along with the flower of Seville's nobility. The Count was only around twenty years old back then, and a long way from the time when, as ninth duke of Medina Sidonia, hounded by the enmity and envy of Olivares and weary of the Crown's rapacious demands on his prosperous estates – whose value had increased due to Sanlúcar de Barrameda's role in the route to and from the Indies – he was drawn into a plot with Portugal to turn Andalusia into an independent kingdom, a conspiracy that brought him dishonour, ruin and disgrace. Behind him came a large retinue of ladies and gentlemen, including the Queen's ladies-in-waiting. And as I searched among them my heart turned over because Angélica de Alquézar was there, exquisitely dressed in yellow velvet trimmed with gold braid, and daintily holding up her skirt, which was held out stiffly by an ample farthingale. Beneath her fine lace mantilla, the same golden ringlets that had brushed my face only hours before gleamed in the afternoon sun. I tried frantically to push my way through the crowd to reach her, but was prevented from doing so by the broad back of a Burgundian guard. Thus Angélica passed by only a few steps away without seeing me. I tried to catch her blue eyes, but she moved off without reading in mine the mixture of reproach and scorn and love and madness that was troubling my mind.

But let us change scenes again, for I promised to tell you about our visit to the royal prison and about Nicasio Ganzúa's final supper. Ganzúa was a prince among outlaws, a notorious ruffian from the quarter known as La Heria. He was a fine example of the criminal classes of Seville and much admired by his fellow ruffians. The next day, to the discordant sound of drums and preceded by a cross, he was to be marched from the prison, then have a rope placed around his neck, a rope that would rob him of his final breath. For this reason, the most illustrious members of the brotherhood of the blade were gathering – with all requisite gravity, stoicism and solemnity – to join him for a final supper. This singular way of bidding farewell to a comrade was known in criminal jargon as *echar tajada*. And it was a common occurrence, for everyone knew that a life of crime or hard graft – the usual term at the time for earning one's living by the sword or by other illicit means – usually ended in the galleys ploughing the seas, hands firmly grasping the neck of an oar beneath the lash of the galley master, or else in a fatal dose of that much more dependable and highly contagious disease, the malady of the rope, a malaise all too widespread amongst rogues.

> *Nothing 'scapes the maw of time,*
> *Scoundrels barely reach their prime*
> *Before the hangman stops their crime.*

A dozen or so inebriated male voices were softly singing these words when at the first watch a constable whose palm had been greased and spirits lifted by Alatriste's bribe of a silver piece of eight led us to the infirmary, which is where they put prisoners about to be executed. Far better pens than mine have described the picaresque life lived within the prison's three gates, barred windows and dark corridors, and the curious reader wishing to know more should turn to Don Miguel de Cervantes, Mateo Alemán or Cristóbal de Chaves. I will merely relate what I saw on that first visit when the doors had been closed and the prisoners who enjoyed the favour of the mayor or of the prison guards and were allowed to come and go as they pleased were all back snug in their cells – apart, that is, from the even more privileged few who, by reason of social position or wealth, could sleep wherever they chose. Wives, whores and relatives had also left the building, and the four taverns and inns that served the prison parish – wine courtesy of the prison governor, water courtesy of the innkeeper – were closed until the following day, as were the gaming tables in the courtyard and the stalls selling food and vegetables. In short, this miniature Spain had gone to sleep, along with the bugs in the walls and the fleas in the blankets, even in the very best cells, which prisoners with the wherewithal could rent for six *reales* a month from the deputy governor, who had bought his post for four hundred ducats from the governor, who, as corrupt

151

as they come, grew rich on bribes and contraband of every sort. As in the rest of Spain, everything could be bought and sold, and you could
rely on money more safely than you could on
justice. All of which only confirmed the truth of
that old Spanish proverb, which says: 'Why go
hungry when it's dark and there are another
man's fig trees to plunder?'

On our way to the supper we had an unexpected
encounter. We had just walked down one long
corridor with bars on either side and past the
women's prison – on the left as one entered –
when we came to a room that was the temporary
home of those about to be sent to the galleys. A
few convicts were standing behind the bars chatting. They peered out at us. A large torch on the
wall lit up that part of the corridor, and by its
light one of the men inside recognised my master.

'Either I'm blind drunk,' he said, 'or that's
Captain Alatriste.'

We paused. The man who had spoken was very
tall and burly, and he had thick black eyebrows
that met in the middle. He was wearing a filthy
shirt and breeches made of rough cloth.

'By the gods, Cagafuego,' said the captain, 'what
are you doing in Seville?'

In his delight and surprise the giant opened his
huge mouth and beamed from ear to ear,
revealing, in place of an upper set of teeth only a
black hole.

'As you can see, they're packing me off to the

galleys. I've got six years of pounding the waves to look forward to.'

'The last time I saw you, you were safe in San Ginés church.'

'Oh, that was a long time ago,' said Bartolo Cagafuego with a stoical shrug. 'You know what life's like.'

'And what crime are you paying for this time?'

'Oh, my crimes and other people's. They say that me and my comrades here' – his comrades smiled fiercely from the back of the cell – 'robbed a few bars in Cava Baja and a few travellers at the Venta de Bubillos, near the Port of Fuenfría . . .'

'So?'

'So, nothing. I didn't have the cash to bribe the scribe with, and once they'd strung me up and plucked me like a guitar, they sent me here to toughen me up for life on the galleys.'

'When did you arrive?'

'Six days ago. After a little jaunt of seventy-five leagues on foot, all of us shackled together, surrounded by guards and in the freezing cold. It was pissing with rain when we reached Adamuz, where we tried to make a run for it, but the catch-poles caught up with us and brought us here. They're taking us down to La Puerta de Santa María on Monday.'

'I'm sorry to hear that.'

'Oh, don't be sorry, Captain. I don't expect much from life, and besides it's all part of the job. And it could have been worse: some of my comrades were sent to the mercury mines in Almadén – that's the real finibusterre, that is. Not many men make it out of there alive.'

'Is there some way I can help?'

Cagafuego lowered his voice.

'If you have a bit of spare cash on you, I'd be very grateful. Me and my friends haven't got a bean.'

Alatriste took out his purse and placed four silver escudos in Cagafuego's great paw.

'How's Blasa Pizorra?'

'Dead, poor woman.' Cagafuego discreetly pocketed the coins, eyeing his companions warily. 'She was taken to the Hospital de Atocha. Her hair had fallen out and she had swellings all over her body. It was dreadful to see her like that, poor thing!'

'Did she leave you anything?'

'Only a sense of relief. She had the pox, of course – hardly surprising given her profession – but by some miracle I never caught it.'

'My condolences anyway.'

'Thank you.'

Alatriste gave a half-smile.

'You never know,' he said 'Perhaps you'll get lucky. The Turks might capture the galley; you might decide to convert and end up in Constantinople in charge of a harem . . .'

'Don't say such things,' said Cagafuego, apparently genuinely offended. 'Let's get this straight: neither the King nor Jesus Christ are to blame for me being where I am now.'

'You're quite right, Cagafuego. I wish you luck.'

'Same to you, Captain Alatriste.'

And he stayed there, leaning against the bars, watching as we walked down the passageway. As I mentioned before, we could hear singing and the strumming of a guitar coming from the infirmary, and the prisoners in nearby cells were now providing an accompaniment, banging knives on bars, clapping and playing improvised flutes. The room set aside for the meal contained a couple of benches and a small altar with a crucifix and a candle, and in the centre was a table adorned with tallow candles and surrounded by several stools, which were occupied at that moment, as were the benches, by a select sample of local ruffians. They had begun arriving at nightfall and continued to do so, grave-faced and solemn, wearing capes thrown back over their shoulders, old buff coats, tow-stuffed doublets – which had been pierced more often than La Méndez herself – hats with the brims turned up at the front, huge curled moustaches, scars, patches, verdigris hearts bearing the names of their lady loves and other such things tattooed on hands and arms, Turkish beards, medallions of Virgins and saints, rosaries of black beads worn around the neck, and all manner of swords and daggers, as well as yellow-handled slaughterer's knives tucked in the legs of gaiters and boots. This dangerous rabble was making short work of the pitchers of wine arranged on the table along with queen olives,

155

capers, Flemish cheese and slices of fried bacon; they addressed each other as 'sir', 'comrade', and 'friend', and spoke with the accents of the criminal classes, mixing up their H's, their J's and their G's, saying for example *gerida* instead of *herida*, *jumo* instead of *humo*, *harro* instead of *jarro*. They toasted the souls of Escamilla and of Escarramán and drank to the soul of Nicasio Ganzúa, the latter still very much there and safely ensconced in its owner's body. They drank as well to the honour of Nicasio himself – 'To your honour, comrade,' cried the ruffians – and every man there would gravely raise his mug to his lips to make the toast. Not even at a wake in Vizcaya or at a Flemish wedding would you see such a thing. And as I watched them drinking and heard them over and over, mentioning Ganzúa's honour, I marvelled that it should be so great.

> *Go for hearts or diamonds*
> *If you seek a winning knave;*
> *Avoid black-hearted spades,*
> *For they will dig your grave.*

The songs continued as did the drinking and the talk, and more comrades kept arriving. Sallow-skinned and menacing, with broad hands and face, and a huge moustache whose ferocious waxed ends reached almost to his eyes, Ganzúa was a strapping man in his late thirties and still as sharp as a razor. He had dressed for the occasion in his

156

Sunday best: a purple slightly darned doublet, slashed sleeves, green canvas breeches, shoes for promenading in and a four-inch-wide belt with a silver buckle. It was a pleasure to see him looking so smart and so solemn, accompanied, encouraged and cheered by his confrères, every one of them wearing a fine hat and looking for all the world like a Spanish grandee, gaily downing the wine, of which several pints had already been drunk and which showed no signs of running out because – not trusting the wine sold by the prison governor – the comrades had brought with them a large supply of pitchers and bottles from a tavern in Calle Cordoneros. As for Ganzúa, he appeared not to be taking his early-morning appointment too much to heart and played his part with courage, decorum and a proper sense of gravity.

'Death, my friends, is of no importance,' he would declare now and then with great aplomb.

Captain Alatriste, who understood this world well, went over and courteously introduced himself to Ganzúa and company, passing on greetings from Juan Jaqueta, whose situation in the Corral de los Naranjos, he explained, meant that he could not have the pleasure of accompanying him that night to bid farewell to his friend. Ganzúa responded equally courteously, inviting us to take a seat, which Alatriste did, having first greeted a few acquaintances who were all busy eating and drinking. Ginesillo el Lindo, a fair-haired elegantly dressed ruffian with an affable look, a dangerous smile and long silky shoulder-length hair *à la milanesa*, greeted him warmly, delighted to see him well and in Seville. Ginesillo was, as everyone knew, effeminate – by which I mean that he had little taste for the act of Venus – but he was as brave as any man and as deadly as a scorpion with a doctorate in the art of fencing. Others of his ilk proved less fortunate, and were arrested on the slightest pretext; they were treated by everyone, even the other prison inmates, with terrible cruelty which only ended when they were burned at the stake. In this frequently hypocritical and contemptible Spain a man could with impunity lie with his own sister or daughters or even his grandmother, but, as with blasphemy and heresy, committing the abominable sin of sodomy meant only one thing: the pyre. By contrast, killing, stealing, corruption and bribery were considered mere bagatelles.

I took my place on a stool, sipped some wine, ate a few capers and listened to the conversation and the solemn arguments that each man offered Nicasio Ganzúa by way of consolation or encouragement. 'Doctors kill more people than the executioner,' one said. Another colleague pointed out that behind every bad lawsuit there's a sly scribe. Another said that death, though a nuisance, was the inevitable fate of all men, even dukes and popes. Someone else cursed the whole race of lawyers, who had no equal, he affirmed, even amongst Turks and Lutherans. 'May God be our judge,' said another, 'and leave justice to the fools.' Yet another regretted that the sentence imposed on Ganzúa would deprive the world of such an illustrious member of the criminal classes.

'My only regret,' said a fellow prisoner who was also at the wake, 'is that my own sentence hasn't been signed yet, although I'm expecting it at any moment. It's a damned shame it didn't arrive today, because then I would gladly have joined you on the scaffold tomorrow.'

Everyone thought this the sentiment of a true comrade and, praising its aptness, pointed out to Ganzúa how much his friends admired him and how honoured they were to be able to keep him company at this time, just as they would the following morning in Plaza de San Francisco – those of them, that is, who could walk the streets without fear of the constables. They would all do the same for each other one day, and whatever trials a fellow ruffian might suffer, he would always have his friends.

'You have to face death with courage, just as you've always faced life,' said a man with a much-scarred face and a fringe as greasy as the collar of his shirt. His name was El Bravo de los Galeones, a sharp-witted rogue from Chipiona.

'On my grandmother's grave, that's true,' replied Ganzúa serenely. 'No one did me a wrong they didn't pay for later, but if I have missed anyone, then come the Resurrection, when I step out into the new world, I'll really let him have it.'

All nodded sagely. This was how real men talked, and they all knew that at his execution the following day Ganzúa would neither blanch nor turn religious. He was after all a brave man and a scion of Seville; everyone knew that La Heria did not breed cowards, and that others before him had drunk from that same cup and never quailed. A man with a Portuguese accent offered the consoling thought that at least the sentence had been imposed by the King's justice, and therefore almost by the King himself, and so it was not just anyone who was taking Ganzúa's life. It would have been a mark of dishonour for such a famous rogue to be dispatched by a nobody. This remark was roundly applauded by the other men there, and Ganzúa smoothed his moustache, pleased with such a measured assessment of the situation. The idea had come from a ruffian in a knee-length buff coat; he had little fat on him and little hair, and what hair he did have grew grey and curly and thick around the noble bronzed dome of his head. It was said that he'd been a theologian at Coimbra University until some misfortune had set him on the path of crime. Everyone considered him to be a man of the law and of letters as well as a swordsman. He was known as Saramago el Portugués, had a stately air about him and was said to kill only out of necessity, hoarding all his money like a Jew in order to print, at his own expense, an endless epic poem on which he'd been working for the last twenty years in which he described how the Iberian Peninsula broke away from Europe and drifted off like a raft on the ocean, crewed entirely by the blind. Or something like that.

'It's my Maripizca I feel sorry for,' said Ganzúa between mugs of wine.

Maripizca la Aliviosa was Ganzúa's doxy, and he believed that his execution would leave her all alone in the world. She had come to see him that very evening, crying and weeping – Ah, light of my eyes and love of my life, et cetera – fainting away every five steps or so into the arms of around twenty of the condemned man's comrades. During the tender conversation that followed Ganzúa had apparently commended his soul to her by asking her to pay for a few masses to be said – because a ruffian would never confess, not even on his way to the scaffold, on the grounds that it was dishonourable to go bleating to God about something he had refused to reveal under torture – and to come to some agreement with the executioner, either by offering him money or her body, so that the next day everything would be done in an honourable and dignified fashion, ensuring that he did not cut a foolish figure when the rope was tightened round his neck in Plaza de San Francisco in full view of his acquaintances. La Aliviosa had finally bade him a graceful farewell, praising her man's courage and expressing the hope that she would see him again in the next world, 'looking just as healthy and handsome and brave'.

La Aliviosa, said Ganzúa to his guests, was a good hardworking woman, clean about her person and a good earner too, who only needed the occasional beating to keep her in order. However, there was scarcely any need to praise her further because she was well known to all the men present, indeed to all of Seville and half of Spain. And as for the razor scar on her face, well, it hardly spoiled her appearance at all; besides, Ganzúa had done it while blind drunk on good Sanlúcar oloroso. All couples had their little misunderstandings, didn't they? Indeed, a timely cut to the face was a healthy sign of affection, the proof of this being that whenever he felt obliged to give her a good hiding, his eyes always filled with tears. La Aliviosa had shown herself to be a dutiful faithful companion by taking care of him in prison with money earned by works that would be discounted from her sins, if indeed it was a sin to make sure that the man of her heart lacked for nothing. And that was all there was to be said on the matter. At this point, Ganzúa grew a little emotional, although in a very manly way: he sniffed and took another sip of wine, and various voices chimed in to reassure him. 'Don't worry, she'll come to no harm. I give you my word,' said one. 'Mine too', said another. 'That's what friends are for,' put in a third. Comforted to know that he was leaving her in such good hands, Ganzúa continued drinking while Ginesillo el Lindo warbled a seguidilla or two in tribute to Maripizca.

'As for the grass snake who mentioned my name,' said Ganzúa, 'you will of course take care of him too.'

These words were greeted with another chorus of protests. It went without saying that the snake who had placed Señor Ganzúa in this woeful situation would, at the earliest opportunity, be relieved of both breath and money; his friends owed the prisoner this and more. For the worst sin any ruffian could commit was to squeal on a comrade, and even if that comrade had done said ruffian some offence or harm, it was felt to be entirely unacceptable to betray that person to the law, the chosen option being to remain silent and exact one's own revenge.

'If you can and if it's not too much trouble, get rid of Catchpole Mojarrilla too, will you? He handled me roughly, and showed me no respect.'

Ganzúa could count on it, his friends assured him. They swore on God and all his angels that he could consider Mojarrilla to have received the last rites already.

'It might be a good idea,' added Ganzúa after a moment's thought, 'to send the silversmith my greetings as well.'

The silversmith was added to the list. And while they were on the subject, they agreed that if the following morning the executioner proved not to have been sufficiently rewarded by La Aliviosa and failed to do a decent job by not tightening the garrotte as cleanly and efficiently as required, he too would get his just deserts. It was one thing to execute someone – after all, everyone had his job to do – but quite another, worthy of traitors and pretty boys, not to show due respect for a man of honour, et cetera, et cetera. There were many other remarks in the same vein, and Ganzúa was left feeling both satisfied and comforted. He looked at Alatriste, grateful that he should have come to keep him company.

'I don't believe I've had the pleasure of your acquaintance,' he said.

'Some of the other gentlemen here know me already,' replied the captain. 'And I am pleased to be able to accompany you on behalf of those friends who cannot be here.'

'Say no more.' Ganzúa was looking at me amiably from behind his vast moustaches. 'Is the boy with you?'

The captain said that I was, and I in turn nodded in a courteous way that provoked murmurs of approval from the other men present, for no one appreciates modesty and good manners in the young more than the criminal classes.

'He's a fine-looking lad,' said Ganzúa. 'I hope it will be a long time before he finds himself in my situation.'

'Amen to that,' agreed Alatriste.

Saramago el Portugués also praised my presence there. It was, he remarked, with a Lusitanian slur to his Ss, an edifying spectacle for a young lad to see how men of courage and honour took their

164

leave of this world, especially in these troubled times when shamelessness and ill manners were so rife. Aside from having the good fortune to have been born in Portugal – not alas a possibility open to everyone – nothing was more instructive than to witness a good death, to speak with wise men, to know other lands and to read widely and well. He concluded poetically, 'Thus the boy will be able to say with Virgil, "*Arma virumque cano*," and with Lucan, "*Plus quam civilia campos*."'

This was followed by much talk and more wine. Ganzúa then proposed a last game of cards with his friends, and Guzmán Ramírez, a silent grave-faced ruffian, took a grimy pack from his doublet and placed it on the table. The cards were dealt out to the eight players while others watched and all of us drank. Wagers were made and, whether by luck or because his comrades were letting him win, Ganzúa had some good hands.

'I'll wager six ducats, my life on it.'

'It's your turn to cut the cards.'

'I'll deal.'

'What a hand!'

'I'll buy it from you, if you like.'

And they were happily occupied in this fashion when steps were heard in the passageway and in came the court scribe, the prison governor with his constables and the prison chaplain, all as black as crows, to read the final sentence. Apart from Ginesillo el Lindo, who stopped playing the guitar, no one took the slightest notice; not even the condemned man showed a flicker of interest; instead, they all continued downing their wine, each player holding his three cards and keeping one eye on the card that had just been turned up, which happened to be the two of hearts. The scribe cleared his throat and declared that, according to the King's justice, the prisoner's appeal having been refused on such and such a date for such and such a reason, the aforementioned Nicasio Ganzúa would be executed the following morning. Ganzúa listened impassively, concentrating on his cards, and only when the sentence had been read did he open his mouth to look at his companion and raise his eyebrows.

'I'll see you,' he said.

The game continued as before. Saramago el Portugués put down a jack of clubs, another comrade played a king and another an ace of diamonds.

'The whore of hearts,' announced a comrade known as El Rojo Carmona, placing a card on the table.

'The black deuce,' said another, putting his card down as well.

Luck was with Ganzúa that night because he had a card that beat them all, and with one hand placed defiantly on his hip, he flung down the four of hearts. Only then, while he was picking up the coins and adding them to his pile, did he look up at the scribe.

'Could you repeat what you just said. I wasn't listening.'

The scribe grew angry, saying that such statements could be read only once, and that it was Ganzúa's own fault if, as he put it, he'd blown out the candle without first making sure he'd understood the deal.

'To a man like me,' replied Ganzúa with great aplomb, 'who has never bowed his head except to take communion and then only when I was a boy, and who has since then fought five hundred duels and been in five hundred scraps and fearlessly fought in a thousand more, the details are about as important as a flea bite. All I want to know is do I face execution tomorrow or not?'

'You do. At eight o'clock precisely.'

'And who signed the death sentence?'

'Judge Fonseca.'

Ganzúa gave his companions a meaningful look, and they responded with winks and silent nods. It would seem that the informer, the catchpole and the silversmith would not be making their journey alone.

'The judge,' said Ganzúa philosophically to the scribe, 'is perfectly at liberty to hand down a sentence and take away my life, but if he had the decency to face me sword in hand then we'd see who would take whose life.'

There were more solemn nods from the circle of ruffians. What he had said was as true as the Gospel. The scribe shrugged. The chaplain, an Augustinian friar with a gentle air and filthy fingernails, came over to Ganzúa.

'Do you wish to confess?'

Ganzúa looked at him while he shuffled the cards.

'You wouldn't want me to blurt out now what I refused to reveal under torture.'

'I was referring to your soul.'

Ganzúa touched the rosary and the medallions which he wore around his neck.

'I'll take care of my soul,' he said after a long pause. 'And tomorrow, in the next world, I'll have a few words with the appropriate person.'

His fellow players nodded approvingly. Some had known Gonzalo Barba, a famous rogue who began his confession to a young and inexperienced priest by admitting straight out to eight murders. Seeing the look of alarm on the young priest's face, he had said, 'Honestly, I start with the small stuff, and already you're shocked. If you react like that to the first eight, then I'm not the right man for you, father, and you're not the right man for me.' And when the priest insisted, he added, 'Look at it this way, father. You were ordained the day before yesterday and here you are trying to confess a man with hundreds of murders under his belt.'

They returned to their cards while the friar and the others headed for the door. Just as they were about to leave, however, Ganzúa remembered something and called them back.

'Just one thing, Señor Scribe. Last month, when they tied the rope around my friend Lucas Ortega's neck, one of the steps on the scaffold was loose, and Lucas nearly fell when he was climbing them. It doesn't bother me particularly, but be so kind as to repair it for whoever comes after me, because not all men have my courage.'

'I'll make a note of it,' the scribe assured him.

'I'll say no more then.'

The men of law and the friar left, and those who remained carried on playing cards and drinking while Ginesillo el Lindo resumed his strumming.

Though he killed his father and his mother
And did his elder brother in,
And put two sisters on the game,
They hung him high on the gallows tree
Of old Seville because he stole
The lives of strangers, one, two, three.

The game continued in the grubby light of the tallow candles. The ruffians drank and played, solemnly keeping watch over their comrade with many 'Ye gods' and 'I' faiths' and 'By my troths'.

'It hasn't been a bad life,' Ganzúa suddenly said thoughtfully. 'Hard but not bad.'

Through the window came the sound of the bells of the church of San Salvador. Out of respect, Ginesillo el Lindo stopped his singing and his strumming. Everyone, including Ganzúa, doffed his hat and interrupted the game to make the sign of the cross. It was the Hour of All Souls – midnight.

The next day dawned with a sky worthy of a painting by Diego Velázquez, and in the Plaza de

169

San Francisco Nicasio Ganzúa climbed the steps of the scaffold with great dignity. I went to watch with Alatriste and a few companions from the previous night. We were just in time to get a place because the square was crammed from end to end with people crowding round the platform and filling the surrounding balconies, and it was said that from a shuttered window of the Audiencia even the King and Queen were watching. Country folk and important figures alike had come to see the event, and the best places, which had been hired out for the occasion, gleamed and glittered with the finest materials: ladies' mantillas and skirts, gentlemen's velvets and feathered felt hats and gold chains. The crowd was full of the usual selection of idlers, thieves and ne'er-do-wells, and those skilled in the art of picking pockets were making their fortunes by slipping two sly fingers into other men's purses and drawing out fistfuls of coins. Don Francisco de Quevedo pushed his way through the crowd to join us and was observing the spectacle with keen interest because, he said, the execution would prove useful for a particular passage in *The Swindler*, the book on which he was currently working.

'One doesn't always draw one's inspiration from Seneca or Tacitus,' he explained, adjusting his eyeglasses.

Someone must have told Ganzúa that the King and Queen were there, because when he was brought from the prison dressed in his smock, mounted on a mule, his hands bound in front of him, he raised both hands to his face to smooth his moustaches and even gestured up at the balconies. His hair was combed; he looked clean, elegant and utterly calm, and the only sign of last night's carousing was a slight redness of the eyes. Along the way, whenever he spotted a familiar face amongst the crowd he would wave graciously, as if he were part of a religious procession heading for the Prado de Santa Justa. In short, he bore himself with such grace that it almost made one feel like being executed oneself.

The executioner was waiting beside the garrotte. As Ganzúa slowly climbed the scaffold steps – the rickety step was still rickety, which earned the scribe, who was standing nearby, a stern look – everyone commented on his excellent manners and his courage. With his raised hands he greeted his comrades and La Aliviosa, who was standing right at the front being comforted by some dozen ruffians and who, despite her copious tears, felt proud of how handsome her man looked as he made his way to death. Then Ganzúa allowed the Augustinian friar of the previous night to preach to him a little and nodded solemnly whenever the friar said something pithy or pleasing. The executioner was becoming visibly grumpy and impatient, so Ganzúa told him, 'Don't hurry me. I'll be with you in a moment. After all, the world's not about to end and there are no Moors to fight.' He then recited the Creed from beginning to end in a strong steady voice, kissed the cross with great feeling and asked the executioner to ensure that he placed the hood properly on his head and afterwards wiped any drool from his moustache so that he would not look undignified. When the executioner said the customary words, 'Forgive me, brother, I am only doing my duty,' Ganzúa retorted that he was forgiven from there to Lima, but to make sure he did a good job, because they would see each other in the next life where Ganzúa would have nothing to lose if he took his revenge. Then he sat down and did not flinch or grimace as they placed the rope around his neck, looking instead almost bored. He smoothed his moustaches one last time, and at the second turn of the garrotte his face grew perfectly calm and serene, as if he were sunk in thought.

CHAPTER 7

ALL'S FISH THAT COMES
TO THE NET

The treasure fleet was about to arrive, and Seville, along with all of Spain and Europe, was preparing to make the most of the torrent of gold and silver it was carrying in its holds. The vast squadron now filling the horizon with sails had arrived at the mouth of the Guadalquivir, escorted from the Azores by the Atlantic Armada, and the first galleons, laden almost to the gunwales with merchandise and other riches, were beginning to drop anchor opposite Sanlúcar or in the bay of Cádiz. In gratitude to God for having kept the fleet safe from storms, pirates and the English, the churches were busy organising masses and Te Deums. Shipowners and those employed in unloading the fleet were already counting their profits; merchants were clearing their shops to make room for the new merchandise or arranging for it to be transported elsewhere; bankers were writing to their correspondents to draw up letters of exchange; the King's creditors were drafting invoices which they hoped would soon be paid; and customs clerks were rubbing their hands at the thought of lining their own pockets. All Seville was smartening itself up for the great event; business picked up; crucibles and dies were made ready for minting coins; the two towers, the Torre de Oro and the Torre de Plata, were prepared as storehouses; and El Arenal was a hive of activity, crowded with carts, piles of provisions, curious onlookers and with black and Moorish slaves labouring by the quayside. The doorways of houses and shops were scrubbed and swept; inns, taverns and bawdy houses were spruced up; and everyone, from the proudest aristocrat to the humblest beggar and the oldest jade, rejoiced at the prospect of the fortune in which they all hoped to share.

'You're lucky,' said the Count of Guadalmedina, looking up at the sky. 'You'll have good weather in Sanlúcar.'

That same afternoon, before we set off on our mission – we were to meet the accountant Olmedilla on the pontoon bridge at six o'clock – Guadalmedina and Don Francisco de Quevedo had come to say goodbye to Captain Alatriste. We had met in El Arenal by the wall of the old arsenal, at a small inn constructed out of planks and canvas rifled from the nearby careening wharf. Tables and stools stood outside beneath a makeshift porch. At that hour the inn, frequented only by a few sailors, was quiet and private, a good place for a drink and a chat. It enjoyed a pleasant view too, overlooking the lively port, where longshoremen, carpenters and shipwrights were working on the boats moored on either shore. Triana – all whites and reds and yellow ochres – was resplendent on the far side of the Guadalquivir, with the caravels of the sardine fleet and the little ferry boats coming and going between the two shores, their lateen sails unfurled to catch the late-afternoon breeze.

'Here's to plenty of booty,' said Guadalmedina.

We all raised our mugs and drank. The wine might not have been special, but the occasion was. Don Francisco de Quevedo, who would in a way have liked to join us on that expedition downriver, was irritated by the fact that, for obvious reasons, he could not. He was still very much a man of action, and it would not have bothered him in the least to add the boarding of the *Niklaasbergen* to his other experiences.

'I wish I could have just a glimpse of your recruits,' he said, polishing his spectacles with a handkerchief which he produced from the sleeve of his doublet.

'So do I,' agreed Guadalmedina. 'I'm sure they form a highly picturesque group, but we cannot involve ourselves any further. From now on the responsibility is entirely yours, Alatriste.'

The poet put on his spectacles and twirled his moustache, and a sly look appeared on his face.

'This is so typical of Olivares. If things go well, there will be no need to bestow any public honours, but if things go badly, heads will roll.'

He took two long swigs of wine and stared thoughtfully into his mug.

'Sometimes, Captain,' he said gravely, 'I regret ever having drawn you into this.'

'No one's forcing me to do it,' said Alatriste, expressionless. He was gazing across at the Triana shore.

The captain's stoical remark made the Count smile.

'They say,' he murmured in an insinuating tone, 'that our King Philip knows all about the plan. He's delighted to have this chance to play a trick on the old Duke of Medina Sidonia and to imagine the look on his face when he finds out. And of course gold is gold, and His Catholic Majesty needs it just as much as any other man.'

'Possibly more,' sighed Quevedo.

Guadalmedina leaned across the table and lowered his voice. 'Last night, in circumstances I need not go into here, His Majesty asked who was in charge of the attack.' He left these words hanging in the air for a moment to allow their meaning to penetrate. 'He asked this of a particular friend of yours, Alatriste, and that friend told him all about you.'

'And praised him to the skies, I suppose,' said Quevedo.

The Count shot him a look, offended by that 'I suppose'.

'As I said, he was a friend of the captain.'

'And what did the great Philip say?'

'Being young and adventurous, he showed considerable interest. He even spoke of turning up tonight at the embarkation point – incognito of course – just to satisfy his curiosity. Naturally, Olivares was horrified at the idea.'

An awkward silence fell.

'That's all we need,' commented Quevedo: 'to have the King on our backs.'

Guadalmedina was turning his mug round and round in his hands.

'Whatever happens,' he said after a pause, 'a success would suit us all very well.'

He suddenly remembered something, put his hand inside his doublet and removed a piece of paper folded in four. It bore the seal of the Audiencia Real and another from the master of the King's galleys.

'I was forgetting your safe-conduct pass,' he said, handing it to the captain. 'It authorises you to go downriver to Sanlúcar. Needless to say, once there you must burn the document. From that moment on, if anyone asks why you're going to Sanlúcar, you'll have to find your own excuse.' The Count was smiling and stroking his goatee beard. 'You could always say you're going fishing for tuna and palm them off with that old saying: "All's fish that comes to the net."'

'I wonder how Olmedilla will acquit himself,' said Quevedo.

'There's no need for him actually to board the ship. He's only required to take charge of the gold once it has been unloaded. His well-being depends on you, Alatriste.'

The captain was studying the document.

'I'll do what I can.'

'Please do. For all our sakes.'

The captain tucked the piece of paper into the leather band inside his hat. While he remained as cool and collected as ever, I kept fidgeting about on my stool. There were too many kings and count-dukes involved in this affair for a simple lad like me to be expected to sit still.

'There will of course be protests from the ship's owners,' said the Count. 'Medina Sidonia will be furious, but no one involved in the plot itself will breathe a word. With the Flemish, it will be different. We're sure to have protests from that quarter, exchanges of letters and storms in the chanceries. That's why we need to make it look like a private affair – an attack by bandits or pirates.' He raised his mug of wine to his lips, smiling mischievously. 'Although no one can demand the return of gold that doesn't officially exist.'

'Remember,' said Quevedo to the captain, 'if anything goes wrong, everyone will deny all knowledge of the matter.'

'Even Don Francisco and myself,' added Guadalmedina bluntly.

'Precisely. *Ignoramus atque ignorabimus.*'

The poet and the aristocrat sat looking at Alatriste, but the captain, who was still staring across at the Triana shore, merely gave a brief nod and said nothing.

'If things do go wrong,' went on Guadalmedina, 'be very careful, because there will be Hell to pay. And you will have to cover the cost of any broken pots.'

'If, that is, they catch you,' said Quevedo.

'In short,' concluded the Count, 'under no circumstances must anyone be captured.' He shot me a quick glance. 'No one.'

'Which means,' explained Quevedo with his usual pithiness, 'that there are only two options: you either succeed, or you die with your mouth closed.'

He said this so clearly and frankly that his words barely weighed on me.

After saying goodbye to our friends, the captain and I walked through El Arenal to the pontoon, where the accountant Olmedilla was waiting for us, as punctual and proper as ever. He walked beside us, a thin austere silent figure, dressed all in black. Beneath the slanting rays of the setting sun we crossed the river, heading for the sinister walls of the castle of the Inquisition, a sight that stirred my worst memories. We were all equipped for the journey: Olmedilla was wearing a long black cape, the captain his cloak, hat, sword and dagger, and I was carrying an enormous bundle containing a few provisions, two cotton blankets, a full wineskin, a pair of pistols, my dagger – its hilt having been repaired in Calle Vizcaínos – gunpowder, bullets, Constable Sánchez's sword, my master's buff coat and a newer much lighter one for myself made of good stout buffalo skin, which we had bought for twenty escudos in a shop in Calle Francos. The meeting point was the Corral del Negro near the Cruz del Altozano, and, leaving behind us the bridge and the collection of longboats, galleys and skiffs moored along the shore as far up as the harbour used by the local shrimpers, we reached the Corral just as night was falling. Triana was full of cheap inns, taverns, gaming rooms and places where soldiers congregated, and so there was nothing unusual about the sight of men bearing swords. The Corral del Negro was, it transpired, a vile inn with an open-air courtyard that served as a drinking den, and which on rainy days was covered over with an old awning. People sat out there with their hats down over their eyes and their cloaks wrapped about them, and given that it was a cool night and given the nature of the customers who frequented the inn, it seemed perfectly normal for everyone to have their face covered so that only their eyes were visible, and to wear a dagger in their belt and a sword beneath their cloak. The captain, Olmedilla and I took seats in one corner, ordered some wine and some food and cast a phlegmatic eye around us. Some of our men were already there. At one table I recognised Ginesillo el Lindo – without his guitar this time but with an enormous sword at

180

his belt – and Guzmán Ramírez, both of them with hats pulled down low and cloaks muffling their faces, and a moment later I saw Saramago el Portugués enter alone and take a seat, where, by the light of a candle, he immediately took a book out of his pouch and started reading. Then in came Sebastián Copons, as small, compact and silent as ever. He sat himself down with a pitcher of wine without so much as a glance at anyone, not even his own shadow. Not one of them betrayed by the merest flicker that they knew each other, and gradually, alone and in pairs, the others arrived too, swaggering and shifty-eyed, swords clanking, finding places to sit wherever they could but never saying a word. The largest group to arrive was a threesome: Juan Jaqueta of the long side whiskers, his friend Sangonera and the mulatto Campuzano, who had all been allowed to leave their ecclesiastical seclusion thanks to the opportune intervention of the captain, courtesy of Guadalmedina. Although accustomed to a fairly rough clientele, the innkeeper observed such an influx of ruffians with a suspicion that the captain soon dissipated by placing a few silver coins in his hand, the perfect way to render even the most curious of innkeepers blind, deaf and dumb, as well as acting as a warning that if he talked too much, he might easily end up with his throat neatly slit. Within half an hour the whole crew was assembled. To my surprise, for Alatriste had made no mention of him, the last to arrive was Bartolo

Cagafuego. With his cap low over his bushy brows and wearing a broad smile that revealed his dark toothless mouth, he paced up and down beneath the arcade near our table, winking at the captain and generally behaving about as discreetly as a bear at a requiem mass. My master never passed any comment on the matter, but I suspect that, although Cagafuego was more braggart than blade, and although the captain could doubtless have recruited another man made of sterner stuff, he had arranged for Cagafuego to be set free for sentimental reasons – if such reasons could ever be attributed to the captain. Anyway, there he was, and he could barely conceal his gratitude. And well might he be grateful, for the captain had saved him from six long years chained to an oar in the galleys with a galley master forever yelling at him to row harder and faster.

This completed the group, and no one failed to make the rendezvous. I watched Olmedilla's face to see his reaction to the fruits of the captain's recruitment campaign, and although the accountant maintained his usual cold inexpressive mute facade, I thought I saw a glimmer of approval. Apart from those already mentioned – and as I learned shortly afterwards when told their real or assumed names – there was Pencho Bullas, the man from Murcia, the old soldiers Enríquez el Zurdo and Andresito el de los Cincuenta, the grimy and much-scarred Bravo de los Galeones, a sailor from Triana called Suárez, another called Mascarúa, a very pale

182

hollow-eyed man looking every inch the down-at-heel hidalgo who was known as El Caballero de Illescas, and a rubicund bearded smiling fellow from Jaén with a shaven head and strong arms, Juan Eslava by name, who was notorious in Seville as a pimp. He lived off the earnings of four or five women and cared for them, almost, as if they were his daughters – a fact that justified his sobriquet, earned fair and square, namely the Lothario of the Alameda. Imagine then the scene, dear reader, with all these brave fellows in the Corral del Negro, their faces muffled by cloaks, who, with every movement, gave off the menacing clank of daggers, pistols and swords. If you hadn't known that they were on your side – at least temporarily – you would have been hard put to find your own pulse, because your heart would have stopped beating out of sheer dread. Once this fearsome retinue was assembled, Diego Alatriste put a few coins on the table, and to the great relief of the innkeeper we set off with Olmedilla to the river, through the pitch-black narrow streets. There was no need to look round. From the sound of footsteps echoing at our backs we knew that the recruits were slipping one by one out of the inn door and following us.

Triana slumbered in the darkness, and anyone still up and about prudently stepped out of our path. The waning crescent of the moon was bright enough to provide us with enough light for us to see a boat, sail furled, silhouetted against the shore. There was one lantern lit at the prow and another on land, and two motionless shapes, master and sailor, were waiting on board. Alatriste now stopped, with Olmedilla and me by his side, while the shadows following us gathered around. The captain sent me to fetch one of the lanterns, which I did, placing it at his feet. The tenuous light of the candle lent a gloomier aspect to the group. Faces were barely visible, only the tips of moustaches and beards, the dark shapes of cloaks and hats, and the dull metallic gleam of the weapons the men all carried at their waists. There was a general murmuring and whispering amongst the comrades as they recognised each other, but the captain abruptly silenced them all.

'We will be going downriver to perform a task which I will explain to you once we reach our destination. You have all been paid something in advance, so there is no going back. And I need hardly say that we are all dumb.'

'You don't need to tell *us* that,' said someone. 'More than one of our number has been on the rack and never uttered a word.'

'Yes, but it's always best to make these things clear. Any questions?'

'When do we get the rest of the money?' asked one anonymous voice.

'When we've completed our mission, but in principle the day after tomorrow.'

'Will we be paid in gold again?'

'You certainly will, in double-headed doubloons, just like those you've received in advance.'

184

'Will there be much killing involved?'

I glanced at the accountant Olmedilla, a dark figure in his black cloak, and I noticed that he was scraping at the ground with the tip of his shoe as if embarrassed or far away, thinking of something else. He was after all a man of paper and ink and unaccustomed to certain harsh facts of life.

'I would hardly bother recruiting men of your calibre,' replied Alatriste, 'merely to dance the chaconne.'

There was some laughter and a few appreciative oaths. When all this had died away, the captain pointed to the boat.

'Go on board and make yourselves as comfortable as you can. And from now on consider yourselves part of a militia.'

'What does that mean?'

In the dim light of the lantern, everyone could see the captain resting his left hand, as if casually, on the hilt of his sword. His eyes pierced the darkness.

'It means,' he said slowly, 'that if anyone disobeys an order or even so much as pulls a face, I'll kill him.'

Olmedilla looked hard at the captain. We could hear the whine of a mosquito. Each man was thinking about what the captain had said and resolving not to incur his leader's displeasure. Then, in the silence, not far off, near the boats moored by the bank of the river, came the sound of oars. Everyone turned to look: a small boat had

185

emerged from the shadows. Against the gleam of lights from the far shore we could make out half a dozen oarsmen and three black shapes standing in the prow. In less time than it takes to describe, Sebastián Copons, ever ready, had leapt into action: as if by magic two enormous pistols appeared in his hands, and he trained them on the people in the boat; Captain Alatriste meanwhile had whipped out his sword and was brandishing its bare steel blade.

'All's fish that comes to the net,' said a familiar voice in the darkness.

As if this were a password, both the captain and I relaxed, for I too had been about to reach for my dagger.

'They're friends,' said Alatriste.

This calmed the men; my master sheathed his sword and Copons put away his pistols. The boat had come to shore just beyond the prow of our vessel, and in the faint light of the lantern we could now make out the three men standing up. Alatriste walked past Copons and went over to them. I followed.

'We've come to say goodbye to a friend,' said the same voice.

I had recognised the Count of Guadalmedina's voice. Like his companions, he kept his face almost concealed with cloak and hat. Behind them amongst the oarsmen I caught the glow of slow-burning matches on two harquebuses. The Count's companions were clearly men of a cautious nature.

'We don't have much time,' said the captain bluntly.

'We wouldn't want to get in your way,' replied Guadalmedina, who was still with his companions in the boat. 'You carry on.'

Alatriste looked at the other two men. One was heavily built, a cloak wrapped about his powerful chest and shoulders. The other man was slimmer, and wore a featherless hat and a brownish-grey cloak that covered him from eyes to feet. The captain lingered for a moment longer, studying them. His features were lit by the lantern on the prow of the boat, with his hawk-like profile and moustache glowing almost red in the light, his eyes vigilant beneath the dark brim of his hat, and his hand touching the bright hilt of his sword. In the gloom he cut a sombre menacing figure, and I imagine he must have made the same impression on the men in the boat. Finally, he turned to Copons, who had hung back a little, and to the other members of the group, who were waiting further off, concealed by the darkness.

'Get on board,' he said.

One by one, with Copons at their head, the ruffians filed past Alatriste, the lantern on the prow illuminating each one as he boarded our boat with a great scrape and clang of ironware. Most of the men covered their faces as they passed the light, but others, indifferent or defiant, left them uncovered. Some even stopped to cast a curious glance at the three cloaked figures, who watched this strange procession without uttering a word. The accountant Olmedilla paused for a moment at the captain's side, anxiously observing the men in the other boat as if uncertain whether or not he should speak to them. Finally he decided against doing so, put one leg over the gunwale of our boat and, encumbered by his cape, would have fallen into the water had a pair of strong hands not hauled him on board. The last to get on was Bartolo Cagafuego, who was carrying the other lantern, which he handed to me before clambering on board, making so much clatter that one would have thought he had half of all the steel produced in Vizcaya either buckled to his belt or in his pockets. My master had still not moved, and was watching the men in the other boat.

'There you have it,' he said in the same brusque tone.

'Not a bad troop of men,' commented the tallest and strongest of the three.

Alatriste looked at him, trying to penetrate the gloom. He had heard that voice before. The third man, slimmer and slighter, who was standing between the other man and Guadalmedina and who had watched the embarkation in silence, was now scrutinising the captain's face.

'Well,' he said at last, 'they certainly frighten me.'

He spoke in a neutral well-educated voice, a voice accustomed to being obeyed. When he heard it, Alatriste stood as still as a statue. For a few seconds I could hear his breathing, calm and very slow. Then he put his hand on my shoulder.

'Get on board,' he ordered.

I obeyed, carrying with me our luggage and the lantern. I jumped over the gunwale and took a seat in the prow, among the other men wrapped in their cloaks, who smelled of sweat, iron and leather. Copons made room for me, and I used the bundle as a seat. From there I could see that Alatriste, on the shore, was still looking at the men in the smaller boat. He raised one hand as if to doff his hat, although without completing the gesture – merely touching the brim – then threw his cloak over his shoulder and climbed into our boat.

'Good fishing,' said Guadalmedina.

No one responded. The master of our boat had cast off, and the sailor, once he had rowed us away from the shore, hoisted the sail. And so, with the help of the current and a gentle breeze blowing from the land, our boat slipped silently downriver, cutting through the black water with its tremulous reflection of the scattered lights of Seville and Triana.

There were countless stars in the sky, and the trees and bushes paraded past to right and left like dense dark shadows as we followed the course of the Guadalquivir. Seville was left far behind us, beyond the bends in the river, and the damp night air drenched the wood of the boat and our cloaks. Olmedilla was lying close by me, shivering. I lay contemplating the night, my blanket pulled up to my chin and my head resting on our bundle of provisions, occasionally glancing across at the motionless silhouette of Alatriste, who was sitting in the stern with the master. Above my head the pale smudge of the sail trembled in the breeze, by turns concealing and revealing the tiny luminous points of light that studded the sky.

Almost everyone was silent, a collection of black shapes huddled together in the narrow space of the boat. Apart from the lapping of the water, I could hear the steady breathing of those asleep, as well as loud snores or the occasional whispered comment from those who remained awake. Someone was humming a tune in a high falsetto. Beside me, his hat over his face and wrapped up in his cloak, Sebastián Copons was sleeping soundly.

My dagger was sticking into my ribs, so, in the end, I took it off. For a while, staring up at the stars with wide eyes, I tried to think of Angélica de Alquézar, but her image kept fading, obscured by the uncertainty of what awaited us downriver. I had heard the Count's instructions to the captain, as well as the latter's conversations with Olmedilla, and I knew the broad lines of the planned attack on the Flemish ship. The idea was to board her while she was anchored at Barra de Sanlúcar, cut her moorings and take advantage of the current and the favourable night tide to carry her towards the coast, where we would run her aground and then transport the booty to the beach; there we would be met by an official escort who had been forewarned of our arrival, a picket from the Spanish guard who should, at that very moment, be arriving in Sanlúcar by land and who would discreetly await the right moment to intervene. As for the crew of the *Niklaasbergen*, they were sailors, not soldiers, and besides, we would be taking them by surprise. With regard to their fate, our orders were clear cut: the assault was to look like a bold incursion by pirates. And if there is one certainty in life, it is that the dead do not talk.

It grew colder towards dawn, with the first light illuminating the tops of the poplars that edged the eastern shore. The cold woke some of the men, and they moved closer to each other in search of warmth. Those not sleeping chatted quietly to pass the time, handing round a wineskin. Some men near me were whispering and seemed to assume that I was asleep. Juan Jaqueta, his friend Sangonera and another man were talking about Captain Alatriste.

'He hasn't changed,' Jaqueta was saying. 'He's still the same cool silent son-of-a-mongrel-bitch.'

'Can he be trusted?' asked one.

'Like a papal bull. He was in Seville for a while, living off his sword like the best of them. We spent some time in the Corral de los Naranjos together. He got into trouble in Naples. Killed someone, apparently.'

'They say he's an old soldier and has fought in Flanders.'

'He has,' said Jaqueta, lowering his voice a little. 'Along with that Aragonese fellow asleep over there and the boy. But he fought in the other war too, at Nieuport and Ostend.'

'Is he good with a sword?'

'I'll say. He's clever too and cunning.' Jaqueta stopped speaking to take a swig from the wine-skin; I heard the gurgle of the wine as he poured it into his mouth. 'When he looks at you with those ice-cold eyes of his, you'd better get out of his way and fast. I've seen him skewer and slash and generally do more damage than a bullet through a buff coat.'

There was a pause and more swigs of wine. I imagined they were looking at Alatriste, still sitting motionless in the bow next to the master, who kept his hand on the tiller.

'Is he really a captain?' asked Sangonera.

'I don't think so,' replied his friend. 'But everyone calls him Captain Alatriste.'

'He's certainly a man of few words.'

'Yes, he's the sort who does his talking with his sword. And he's even better at fighting than he is at holding his tongue. I knew someone who was with him on the galleys in Naples ten or fifteen years ago, on a raid in the Constantinople channel. Apparently, the Turks boarded the ship, having first killed most of the crew, and Alatriste and a dozen or so others were forced to retreat, defending the gangway inch by inch, finally holing themselves up on the half-deck, fighting like savages and fending off the Turks with their knives, until they were all either dead or wounded. The Turks were taking them and the ship back up the channel when, as good fortune would have it, two ships from Malta came to their aid and rescued them from life on a Turkish galley.'

'Sounds like a plucky bastard,' said one.

'You bet, comrade.'

'And he's known the rack too, I'll bargain,' added another man.

'That I don't know, but for the moment at least things don't seem to be going too badly for him. If he can spring us from prison and slap a *noli me tangere* on us, he's obviously got some influence.'

'Who were those three men in the other boat?'

'No idea. But they smelled like important people to me. Perhaps they're the ones supplying the lucre.'

'And what about the man in black? I mean the clumsy clod who almost fell in the water?'

'No idea, but if he's a fellow ruffian, my name's Luther.'

There were more gurgling sounds of wine being drunk followed by a couple of satisfied belches.

'Not a bad job so far, though,' said someone after a while. 'Plenty of gold and good company too.'

Jaqueta chuckled.

'Yeah, but you heard what the boss said. First we have to earn it. And they're not going to give us the money just for strolling up and down of a Sunday.'

193

'Oh, I can live with that,' said one. 'For one thousand two hundred *reales*, I'd steal the morning star.'

'Me too,' agreed another.

'Besides, he certainly deals a fair hand – I'd be happy to have a few more gold 'uns like the ones I've got in my pocket right now.'

I heard them whispering. Those who knew how to add up were busy making calculations.

'Is it a fixed amount?' asked Sangonera. 'Or will they share out the total amongst those who survive?'

Jaqueta gave the same low chuckle.

'We won't find out until afterwards. It's a way of making sure that in the heat and noise of the fighting we don't stab each other in the back.'

The horizon was growing red behind the trees, allowing glimpses of scrub and of the pleasant orchards that sometimes grew as far down as the banks of the river. In the end I got up and made my way past the sleeping bodies to the stern, to join the captain. The master of the boat, who wore a serge smock and a faded cap on his head, declined when I offered him some wine from the skin I'd brought for the captain. He was leaning one elbow on the tiller, intent on estimating the distance from the banks, on the breeze filling the sail and on any loose logs that might be swept up by the waters. He had a tanned face, and until then, I hadn't heard him say a word; nor would

I thereafter. Alatriste took a draught of wine and ate the proffered piece of bread and cured meat. I stayed by his side, watching the cloudless sky and the light as it grew brighter on the horizon. On the river everything was still grey and hazy, and the men lying in the bottom of the boat remained immersed in darkness.

'How's Olmedilla doing?' asked the captain, looking across to where the accountant lay.

'He's finally managed to fall asleep after spending all night shivering.'

My master gave a faint smile. 'He's not used to this kind of thing,' he said.

I smiled too. We were used to it, he and I.

'Is he coming aboard the *urca* with us?'

Alatriste shrugged. 'Who knows?' he said.

'We'll have to look out for him,' I murmured, somewhat concerned.

'Every man will have to look out for himself. When the moment comes, you just worry about yourself.'

We fell silent, passing the wineskin from one to the other. My master chewed on his bread for a while.

'You've grown up a great deal,' he said between mouthfuls.

He was still watching me thoughtfully. I felt a sweet wave of satisfaction warm my blood.

'I want to be a soldier,' I blurted out.

'I thought you'd have had enough after Breda.'

'No, that's what I want to be. Like my father.'

He stopped chewing and studied me a moment longer; then he gave a lift of his chin, indicating the men lying in the boat.

'It's hardly a great future,' he said.

We remained for a while without talking, rocked by the swaying of the boat. Now the landscape behind the trees was growing red and the shadows less grey.

'Besides,' said Alatriste suddenly, 'it'll be a couple of years before they let you join a company. And we've been neglecting your education. So, the day after tomorrow—'

'I read well,' I said, interrupting him. 'I have a reasonably neat hand; I know the Latin declensions and how to add, subtract, multiply and divide.'

'That's not enough. Master Pérez is a good man and he can complete your education once we're back in Madrid.'

He fell silent again and cast another glance at the sleeping men. The easterly light emphasised the scars on his face.

'In this world,' he said at last, 'the pen can sometimes take you places the sword cannot.'

'Well, it's not fair,' I retorted.

'. . . Possibly not.'

He had taken a while to respond, and I thought there was a measure of bitterness in that 'Possibly not'. For my part, I merely shrugged beneath my blanket. At sixteen I was sure that I would go wherever I needed to go and arrive wherever I needed to arrive. And as far as I was concerned Master Pérez had nothing to do with that.

'It isn't the day after tomorrow yet, Captain.'

I said this with something like relief, defiantly, staring obstinately at the river ahead. I didn't need to turn round to know that Alatriste was watching me closely, and when I did turn my face, I saw that his sea-green eyes were tinged with red from the rising sun.

'You're right,' he said, handing me the wineskin. 'We still have a long way to go.'

CHAPTER 8

BARRA DE SANLÚCAR

The sun was directly above us as we passed the inn at Tarfia, where the Guadalquivir turns westwards and you begin to see the marshlands of Doña Ana on the right-hand bank. The fertile fields of Aljarafe and the leafy shores of Coria and Puebla slowly gave way to sand dunes, pine woods and dense scrub out of which emerged the occasional fallow deer or wild boar. It grew hotter and more humid, and in the boat the men folded up their cloaks, unclasped capes and unbuttoned buff coats and doublets. They were crammed together like herrings in a barrel, and the bright light of day revealed scarred and ill-shaven faces as well as ferocious beards and moustaches that did little to belie the piles of weapons, leather belts and baldrics, the swords, half-swords, daggers and pistols that each of them kept nearby. Their grubby clothes and skin – made grimy by the elements, lack of sleep and the journey – gave off a raw rough smell which I knew so well from Flanders. It was the smell of men at war. The smell of war itself.

I sat slightly apart with Sebastián Copons and

the accountant Olmedilla, for although the latter was as aloof as ever, I nevertheless felt a moral obligation, among such a rabble, to keep an eye on him. We shared the wine and the provisions, and although neither Copons, the old soldier from Huesca, nor the functionary from the royal treasury were men of many – or indeed few – words, I stayed close by them out of a sense of loyalty – to Copons because of our shared experiences in Flanders and to Olmedilla because of the particular circumstances in which we found ourselves. As for Captain Alatriste, he spent the twelve leagues of the journey in his own fashion, seated in the stern with the master of the boat, occasionally dropping asleep but only for a few minutes at a time and otherwise barely taking his eyes off the other men. When he did sleep, he lowered his hat over his face, in order, it seemed, not to be seen to be slumbering. When awake, he studied each man carefully in turn, as if he had the ability to delve into their virtues and their vices and thereby know them better. He watched how they ate, yawned, slept, how they reacted – phlegmatically or with ill humour – as each was dealt a hand from Guzmán Ramírez's deck of cards, gambling away money they did not yet have. He noticed who drank a lot and who drank little, who was talkative, who boastful and who silent; he noticed Enríquez el Zurdo's oaths, the mulatto Campuzano's thunderous laugh and the stillness of Saramago el Portugués, who spent the whole voyage lying on his cape, serenely reading a book. Some were silent or discreet like El Caballero de Illescas, the sailor Suárez or the Vizcayan Mascarúa, while others seemed awkward and out of place, like Bartolo Cagafuego, who knew no one and kept making repeated and abortive attempts to strike up conversations. There was no shortage of witty and amusing talkers, such as Pencho Bullas or the ever-cheerful ruffian Juan Eslava, who was regaling his fellows with details of how he personally had benefited from the wonders of powdered rhinoceros horn. Then there were the pricklier characters like Ginesillo el Lindo, with his immaculate appearance, equivocal smile and dangerous gaze, or Andresito el de los Cincuenta, who had a way of spitting out of the side of his mouth, or mean bastards like El Bravo de los Galeones, his face criss-crossed with scars that were clearly not just the work of a particularly careless barber. And so while our boat sailed downriver, one man would be telling tales of his adventures with women or at the gaming table, another would be roundly cursing as he threw dice to pass the time, and yet another would be retailing anecdotes, true or false, from some hypothetical soldier's life that embraced the Battle of Roncesvalles and even took in a couple of campaigns fought under the leadership of the Lusitanian Viriathus. And all of this was spiced with large doses of oaths, curses, braggartry and hyperbole.

'I swear by Christ that I'm a Christian as pure

of blood and as noble as the King himself,' I heard one man say.

'Well, I, by God, am purer than that,' retorted another. 'After all, the King is half Flemish.'

To hear them, you would have thought our boat was filled with the very cream of Aragon, Navarre and the two Castiles, Old and New. This was a coinage common to every purse, and even in such a restricted space and among such a small group as ours, each man played the part of a proud distinguished native of this region or that, one side joining forces against another, with Extremadurans, Andalusians, Vizcayans or Valencians taking it in turns to heap reproaches on each other, brandishing the vices and misfortunes of every province, with much banter and joking, and all agreeing on one thing – their shared hatred of the Castilians – and every man presuming to be a hundred times worthier than he actually was. This gang of roughs thrown together by chance was like Spain in miniature, for the gravity and honour and national pride depicted in the plays of Lope, Tirso and others had vanished with the old century and now existed only in the theatre. All that remained was arrogance and cruelty, and when you considered the high regard in which we held ourselves, our violent customs and our scorn for other provinces and nations, one could understand why the Spanish were, quite rightly, hated throughout Europe and half the known world.

Our own expedition naturally enjoyed its share

of these vices, and virtue would have been about as natural a sight as the Devil plucking a harp, wearing a halo and a pair of white wings. But however nasty, cruel and boastful our fellow travellers were, they nonetheless had certain things in common: they were bound by their greed for the promised gold; their baldrics, belts and sheaths were kept oiled and polished with professional care; and their burnished weapons glinted in the sunlight when they took them out to sharpen or clean them. Accustomed as he was to these people and this life, Captain Alatriste was doubtless coolly comparing these men with others he had known in other places, and would thus be able to guess or foresee how each man would react when night fell. He could, in other words, tell who would be worthy of his trust and who would not.

It was still light when we rounded the final long bend of the river, on the banks of which rose the white mountains of the salt marshes. Between the sandy shore and the pine woods we could see the port of Bonanza, its bay already crowded with moored galleys and ships, and further off, clearly visible in the afternoon sun, stood the tower of the Iglesia Mayor and the tallest of Sanlúcar de Barrameda's houses. Then the sailor furled the sail, and the master steered the boat towards the opposite shore, seeking out the right-hand margin of that broad current which, a league and a half downstream, would flow out into the sea.

We disembarked – getting our feet wet in the process – in the shelter of a large dune that reached its tongue of sand down into the river. Three men watching from a clump of pines came to meet us. They were dressed in dun-coloured clothes, like hunters, but as they approached, we saw that their swords and pistols were hardly of the kind one would use to go hunting rabbits. Olmedilla greeted the apparent leader, a man with a ginger moustache and a military bearing which his rustic outfit did little to disguise. While they withdrew to converse in private, our troop of men clustered together in the shade of the pines. We lay for a while on the needle-carpeted sand watching Olmedilla, who was still talking and occasionally nodding impassively. Now and then the two men would look across at a raised area of land further off, around five hundred paces along the river-bank, and about which the man with the ginger moustache seemed to be giving detailed explanations. Olmedilla finally bade farewell to the supposed hunters, who, after casting an inquisitive glance in our direction, set off into the pines; the accountant then rejoined us, moving across the sandy landscape like some strange black smudge.

'Everything is in place,' he said.

Then he took my master aside and they spoke together for a while in low voices. Sometimes, while he was talking, Alatriste stopped staring down at his boots and would look across at us. Finally Olmedilla fell silent, and I saw the captain ask two questions to which the accountant replied twice in the affirmative. Then they crouched down, Alatriste took out his dagger and started tracing lines with it in the sand, and whenever he glanced up to ask Olmedilla something, the later nodded again. All of this took some time, and afterwards the captain stood quite still, thinking. Then he rejoined us and explained how we were to attack the *Niklaasbergen*. He did this succinctly, with no superfluous comments.

'We'll split into two groups, one per boat. The first group will attack the quarterdeck, trying to make as much noise as possible, but there must be no firing of guns. We will leave our pistols here.'

There was some murmuring, and a few of the men exchanged disgruntled looks. A timely pistol shot meant you could kill a man straight off, more quickly than with a sword and from a safe distance too.

The captain went on: 'We're going to be fighting in the dark and at very close quarters, and I don't want us killing each other by mistake. Besides, if someone's pistol should go off accidentally, they'll fire on us with their harquebuses from the galleon before we've even climbed on board.'

He paused, quietly observing the men.

'Who amongst you has served the King?'

Almost everyone raised his hand. Grave-faced and with his thumbs hooked in his belt, Alatriste studied them one by one. His voice was as ice-cold as his eyes.

'I mean those of you who really have fought as soldiers.'

Many hesitated, embarrassed and looking around shiftily. A couple of men put their hands down, but others kept them up, until, under Alatriste's sustained gaze, they too lowered their hands. Only Copons, Juan Jaqueta, Sangonera, Enríquez el Zurdo and Andresito el de los Cincuenta kept their hands up. Alatriste also picked out Eslava, Saramago el Portugués, Ginesillo el Lindo and the sailor Suárez.

'These nine men will form the group who will attack from the bow. In order to take the crew by surprise and from behind, you will only board the ship once those at the stern are already fighting on the quarterdeck. The idea is that you board very quietly, via the anchor, make your way along the deck and then we will all meet up at the stern.'

'Is there someone in charge of each group?' asked Pencho Bullas.

'There is: Sebastián Copons at the bow and myself at the stern with you, Cagafuego, Campuzano, Guzmán Ramírez, Mascarúa, El Caballero de Illescas and El Bravo de los Galeones.'

I looked from one man to another, confused at first. The difference in the quality of the two groups was glaringly obvious. Then I realised that Alatriste was placing the best men under Copons's command and keeping the least disciplined or least trustworthy for himself, with the exception perhaps of the mulatto Campuzano and possibly

Bartolo Cagafuego, who despite being more braggart than brave, would fight well under the captain's gaze, if only out of a sense of obligation. This meant that the group attacking the bow was the one that would decide the battle, while those at the stern – mere cannon fodder – would bear the brunt of the fighting. And if things went wrong or those boarding at the bow were delayed, the group at the stern would also suffer the greatest losses.

'The plan,' Alatriste went on, 'is to cut the anchor chain so that the ship drifts towards the coast and runs aground on one of the sandbanks opposite San Jacinto Point. For that purpose, the group at the bow will carry with them two axes. We will all remain on board until the ship touches bottom on the bar. Then we will come ashore – the water there is only chest deep – and leave the matter in the hands of others who will be waiting.'

The men again exchanged looks. From the pine woods came the monotonous whirr of cicadas. Apart from the buzz of flies swarming about our heads, that was the only sound to be heard while each man pondered.

'Will there be much resistance?' asked Juan Jaqueta, pensively chewing the ends of his moustache.

'I don't know, but we certainly expect there to be some.'

'How many heretics are there on board?'

'They're not heretics, they're Flemish Catholics,

but it amounts to the same thing. We estimate between twenty and thirty, although many will jump overboard. And there is one important point: as long as there are still crew members alive, not one of us must utter a word of Spanish.' Alatriste looked at Saramago el Portugués, who was listening intently with the grave demeanour of a scrawny hidalgo, a book, as usual, stuffed into the pocket of his doublet. 'It would not go amiss if this gentleman here were to shout something in his own language, and for those of you who know English or Flemish words to let fly with those as well.' The captain allowed himself the flicker of a smile. 'The idea is . . . that we are pirates.'

This remark eased the tension. There was laughter and the men shared amused looks. Amongst such a band of men, this idea was not so very far from the truth.

'And what about those who don't jump over-board?' asked Mascarúa.

'No crew member will reach the sandbank alive. The more people we frighten at the beginning, the fewer we will have to kill.'

'And what about the wounded or those who cry for mercy?'

'Tonight there is no mercy.'

Some whistled through their teeth. There was mocking applause and subdued laughter.

'And what about our own wounded?' asked Ginesillo el Lindo.

'They will leave the ship with us and be attended

to on land. There we will all be paid, and after that it will be a matter of every owl to his olive tree.'

'And if there are deaths?' El Bravo de los Galeones had a smile on his scarred face. 'Do we still earn the same amount each or divide what's left between us?'

'We'll see.'

The ruffian glanced at his comrades and his smile grew wider.

'Perhaps it would be a good idea if we could see right now,' he said pointedly.

Alatriste slowly removed his hat and smoothed his hair. Then he put his hat on again. The way he looked at the other man left no room for doubt.

'Good? For whom exactly?'

He said these words softly, almost in a drawl, in a tone of solicitous enquiry that would not have fooled even a babe in arms. It certainly did not fool El Bravo de los Galeones, for he got the message, averted his eyes and said no more. Olmedilla had sidled up to the captain and was whispering something in his ear. My master nodded.

'This gentleman has just reminded me of another important point. No one, absolutely no one,' said Alatriste, fixing his icy gaze on each man in the group in turn, 'will, for any reason, go down into the ship's hold. There will be no taking of personal booty, none at all.'

Sangonera raised his hand and asked, 'And what if a crew member holes himself up in there?'

'Should that happen, then I will decide who goes down to fetch him.'

El Bravo de los Galeones was thoughtfully stroking his hair, which he wore caught back in a greasy pigtail. Then he asked the question that was on everyone's mind: 'And what is there in this "tabernacle" that we can't see?'

'That's none of your business. It's not even my business. And I hope not to have to remind anyone of that.'

El Bravo gave a jeering laugh.

'Not if my life depended on it.'

Alatriste stared at him hard.

'It does.'

'Now you're going too far, by God.' El Bravo was standing legs apart, shifting his weight from one to the other. 'By my faith, we're not a load of sheep to put up with being threatened like that. Me and my comrades here—'

'I don't give a damn what you can and can't put up with,' Alatriste broke in. 'That's the way it is. You were all warned, and there's no going back.'

'And what if we want to go back?'

'You talk boldly enough in the plural, I see.' The captain ran two fingers over his moustache then pointed to the pine wood. 'As for the singular you, I would be happy to discuss the matter alone, just the two of us, in that wood.'

The ruffian made a silent appeal to his comrades. Some regarded him with what seemed like a glimmer of solidarity, but others did not. For his part, Bartolo Cagafuego had stood up, brows beetling, and was approaching menacingly in support of the captain. I too had reached for my dagger. Most of the men looked away, half smiling or watching as Alatriste's hand brushed the hilt of his sword. No one appeared bothered by the prospect of a good fight, with the captain in charge of the fencing lessons. Those who knew Alatriste's past record had already informed the others, and El Bravo de los Galeones, with his low arrogance and ridiculous swagger – hardly necessary amongst such a crew – was not much liked.

'We'll talk about it some other time,' he said at last.

He had thought it over and preferred not to lose face. Some of his fellow ruffians nudged each other, disappointed that there would be no fight in the woods that afternoon.

'Yes, let's do that,' replied Alatriste gently, 'whenever you like.'

No one said anything more; no one took him up on his offer or even looked as if he would. Peace was restored, Cagafuego's brows unbeetled, and everyone went about his own business. Then I noticed Sebastián Copons withdrawing his hand from the butt of his pistol.

The flies buzzed round our faces as we peered cautiously over the top of the dune. Before us lay Barra de Sanlúcar, brightly lit by the evening sun. Between the inlet at Bonanza and Chipiona Point about a league further on, where the Guadalquivir flowed into the sea, the mouth of the river was a forest of masts with flags flying and the sails of ships – *urcas*, frigates, caravels, small vessels and large, both ocean-going and coastal – either anchored amongst the sandbanks or in constant movement back and forth, this same panorama stretching eastwards along the coast towards Rota and the Bay of Cádiz. Some ships were waiting for the rising tide in order to travel up to Seville, others were unloading merchandise onto smaller boats or adjusting their rigging to sail on to Cádiz once royal officials had checked their cargo. On the far shore we could see, in the distance, prosperous Sanlúcar with its houses reaching right down to the water's edge and on top of the hill the old walled enclave, the castle turrets, the ducal palace, the cathedral and the customs house, which on days such as this brought wealth to so many. The harbour sands were speckled with beached fishing boats, and the lower city, gilded by the sun, teemed with people, with the small sailing boats that came and went between the ships bobbing in the foreground.

'There's the *Virgen de Regla*,' said Olmedilla.

He lowered his voice when he spoke, as if we might be heard on the other side of the river, and wiped the sweat from his face with an already sodden handkerchief. He seemed even paler than usual. He was not a man for long walks or traipsing over sand dunes and through scrub, and the effort and the heat were beginning to take their toll. His ink-stained forefinger was pointing out a large galleon anchored between Bonanza and Sanlúcar, sheltering behind a sandbank just beginning to be revealed by the low tide. Its prow was facing into the southerly breeze that was rippling the surface of the water.

'And that,' he said, pointing to another ship moored closer to us, 'is the *Niklaasbergen*.'

I followed Alatriste's gaze. With the brim of his hat shading his eyes from the sun, the captain was scrutinising the Dutch galleon. It was anchored separately, near our shore, towards San Jacinto Point and the watchtower that had been erected there to prevent incursions by Berber, Dutch and English pirates. The *Niklaasbergen* was a tarblack, three-masted *urca*, or merchant ship, and its sails were furled. It was a short ugly rather clumsy-looking vessel, with a high prow above which hung a lantern painted in white, red and yellow, a perfectly ordinary cargo ship that would not attract attention. Its prow was also facing south and its gunports had been left open to air the lower decks. There appeared to be little movement on board.

'It was anchored next to the *Virgen de Regla* until daybreak,' explained Olmedilla. 'Then it went and dropped anchor over there.'

The captain was studying each detail of the landscape, like a bird of prey that would only be able to pounce on its victim in the dark.

'Is all the gold on board?' he asked.

'No, one part is missing. They chose not to remain moored next to the other ship because they were afraid it might look suspicious. The rest will be brought over by boat at nightfall.'

'How much time do we have?'

'It doesn't set sail until tomorrow, with the high tide.'

Olmedilla indicated the rubble of a ruined netting shed on the shore. Beyond it could be seen a sandy bank which the low tide had left uncovered.

'That's the place,' he said. 'Even at high tide you can wade ashore.'

Alatriste screwed up his eyes even more tightly. He was studying the black rocks barely covered by water, a little further in shore.

'I remember those shallows well,' he said. 'The galleys always did their best to avoid them.'

'I don't think they need worry us,' replied Olmedilla. 'At that hour the tide, the breeze and the river current will all be working in our favour.'

'I certainly hope so. Because if instead of running into the sand, our keel collides with those rocks, we'll go straight under . . . and the gold will go with us.'

We crawled back, keeping our heads down, to join the rest of the men. They were lying on cloaks and capes, waiting with the stolid patience of their profession; and without anyone having said a word they had instinctively gathered into the two groups they would form when it came to boarding the ship.

The sun was disappearing behind the pine woods. Alatriste went and sat on his cloak, picked up the wineskin and drank from it. I spread my blanket on the ground beside Sebastián Copons; Copons was lying on his back, dozing, with a handkerchief covering his face to keep off the flies and his hands folded over the hilt of his dagger. Olmedilla came over to the captain. His fingers were interlaced and he was twiddling his thumbs.

'I'm going with you,' he said softly.

Alatriste, about to take another drink from the wineskin, stopped and regarded him intently.

'That's not a good idea,' he said after a pause.

With his pale skin, sparse moustache and beard unkempt after the journey, the accountant cut a frail figure. However, he insisted, tight-lipped: 'It's my duty. I'm the King's agent.'

The captain thought for a moment, wiping the wine from his moustache with the back of his hand. Then he placed the wineskin on the sand.

'As you wish,' he said suddenly. 'I never meddle in matters of duty.'

He remained thoughtful, though, and silent. Then, with a shrug of his shoulders, he announced, 'You'll board at the bow.'

'Why can't I go with you?'

'We don't want to put all our eggs in one basket, do we?'

Olmedilla shot me a glance, which I held unblinking.

214

'And the boy?'

Alatriste looked at me as if indifferent, then unbuckled the belt bearing his sword and dagger and wrapped the belt around them. He placed this bundle beneath the folded blanket that served as his pillow and unfastened his doublet.

'Íñigo goes with me.'

He lay down to rest with his hat over his face. Olmedilla again interlaced his fingers and resumed his thumb-twiddling. He seemed less impenetrably impassive than usual, as if an idea he could not quite bring himself to express were going round and round in his head.

'And what will happen,' he said at last, 'if the group boarding at the bow is delayed and fails to reach the quarterdeck in time? I mean . . . what if something should happen to you?'

Beneath the hat hiding his face, Alatriste did not stir.

'In that case,' he said, 'the *Niklaasbergen* will no longer be my problem.'

I fell asleep. I closed my eyes as I often had in Flanders before a march or a battle and made the most of what time there was to gather my strength. At first I fell into a superficial doze, opening eyes and ears from time to time to the fading daylight, the bodies lying around me, their breathing and their snores, the murmured conversations and the motionless shape of the captain with his hat over his face. Then I fell into a deeper sleep and allowed myself to float on the gentle black water, adrift on a vast sea filled, as far as the horizon, with innumerable sails. Then Angélica de Alquézar appeared, as she had so many times before. And this time I plunged into her eyes and felt again the sweet pressure of her lips on mine. I looked around for someone to whom I could shout my joy, and there they were, lying still amongst the dank mists of a Flemish canal: the shadows of my father and Captain Alatriste. I squelched through the mud to join them, ready to unsheathe my sword and fight the vast army of ghosts clambering out of tombs: dead soldiers in rusty breastplates and helmets, brandishing weapons in their bony hands and staring at us from hollow sockets. And I opened my mouth to cry out in silence – old words that had lost their meaning because time was plucking them from me, one by one.

I awoke with Captain Alatriste's hand on my shoulder. 'It's time,' he whispered, almost brushing my ear with his moustache. I opened my eyes to the darkness. No one had lit fires, and there were no lanterns. The slender waning moon shed only enough light for me to be able to make out the vague black shapes moving around me. I heard swords being slipped out of sheaths, belts being buckled, hooks fastened, short muttered sentences. The men were preparing themselves, exchanging hats for kerchiefs tied around their heads and wrapping their weapons in cloth so that there would be no telltale clank of metal. As the captain had ordered, all pistols were left on the beach along with the other baggage. We were to board the *Niklaasbergen* armed only with swords and daggers.

I fumbled open our bundle of clothes and donned my new buff coat, still stiff and thick enough to protect my upper body from knife thrusts. Then I made sure my sandals were firmly tied on, that my dagger was securely attached to my belt with a length of cord wound around the hilt, and finally I placed the stolen constable's sword in my leather baldric. All around me men were speaking softly, taking one last swig from the wineskins and relieving themselves before going into action. Alatriste and Copons were standing, heads close together, as the latter received his final instructions. When I stepped back, I bumped into Olmedilla, who recognised me and gave me a little pat on the back, which in a man of such sourness might be considered an expression of affection. I saw that he too was wearing a sword at his waist.

'Let's go,' said Alatriste.

We set off, our feet sinking into the sand. I could identify some of the shadows who passed me: the tall slender figure of Saramago el Portugués, the heavy bulk of Bartolo Cagafuego, the slight silhouette of Sebastián Copons. Someone made a derisory remark, and I heard the muffled laughter of the mulatto Campuzano. The captain's voice boomed out, demanding silence, and after that no one spoke.

As we passed the wood I heard the braying of a mule and, curious, peered into the dark. There were mules and horses hidden amongst the trees and the indistinct shapes of people standing next to them. These were doubtless the men who, later on, when the galleon had foundered on the bar, would be in charge of unloading the gold. As if to confirm my suspicions, three black silhouettes emerged from behind the pines, and Olmedilla and the captain paused to hold a whispered conversation with them. I thought I recognised the 'hunters' we had seen earlier. Then they vanished, Alatriste gave an order, and we set off again. Now we were climbing the steep slope of a dune, plunging in up to our ankles, the outlines of our bodies standing out more clearly against the pale sand. At the top the sound of the sea reached us and the breeze caressed our faces. As far as the horizon, as black as the sky itself, stretched a long dark stain filled with the tiny luminous dots of ship's lanterns, so that it seemed as if the stars were reflected in the sea. Far off, on the other shore, we could see the lights of Sanlúcar.

We went down to the beach, the sand dulling the sound of our steps. Behind me I could hear the voice of Saramago el Portugués, reciting softly to himself:

'But staying with the pilots on the sand,
And being eager to determine where I stand,

218

I pause and calculate the bright sun's height
Then mark our spot, exactly, on the chart.'

Someone asked what the Devil he was mumbling about, and Saramago responded calmly, in his soft cultivated Portuguese voice, that he was reciting some lines from Camões, which made a change from those wretches Lope and Cervantes, that before he went into battle he always recited whatever came into his heart, and that if anyone was affronted to hear a few lines from *The Lusiads* he would be more than happy to fight it out with him *and* his mother.

'That's all we need,' muttered someone.

There were no further comments. Saramago el Portugués resumed his mumbled recitation, and we continued on. Next to the cane fence surrounding the tidal pool created by the fishermen for their fish stocks we saw two boats waiting with a man in each. We gathered expectantly on the shore.

'The men in my group, come with me,' said Alatriste.

He was hatless but had now donned his buff coat, and his sword and dagger hung at his belt. The men duly divided into their allotted groups. They exchanged farewells and wishes of good luck, even the odd joke and the inevitable boasts about how many men they intended to relieve of their souls. There were also cases of ill-disguised nerves, stumblings in the dark and curses.

219

Sebastián Copons walked past us, followed by his men.

'Give me a little time,' the captain said to him in a low voice. 'But not too much.'

Copons gave his usual silent nod and waited as his men climbed into the boat. The last to embark was the accountant Olmedilla. His black clothes made him seem darker still. He splashed about heroically in the water, tangled up in his own sword, while they helped him in.

'And take care of that one, too, if you can,' Alatriste added to Copons.

'God's teeth, Diego,' replied Copons, who was tying his neckerchief around his head. 'That's too many orders for one night.'

Alatriste chuckled. 'Who would have thought it, eh, Sebastián? Cutting Flemish throats in Sanlúcar.'

Copons grunted. 'Well, when it comes to cutting throats, one place is as good as any other.'

The group assigned to the attack on the bow was also embarking. I went with them, wading into the water, then scrambled over the edge of the boat and sat down on a bench. A moment later the captain joined us.

'Start rowing,' he said.

We tied the oars to the tholes and began rowing away from the shore while the sailor took the tiller and guided us towards a nearby light that shimmered on the water ruffled by the breeze. The other boat remained a silent presence close by, the oars entering and leaving the water as quietly as possible.

'Slowly now,' said Alatriste, 'slowly.'

Seated next to Bartolo Cagafuego, my feet resting on the bench in front of me, I bent forward with each stroke then threw my body back, pulling hard on the oar. Thus the end of each movement left me staring up at the stars that shone brightly in the vault of the sky. As I bent forward I sometimes turned and looked back past the heads of my comrades. The lantern at the galleon's stern was getting closer.

'So,' muttered Cagafuego to himself, 'I didn't escape the galleys after all.'

The other boat began to move away from us, with the small figure of Copons standing up in the prow. It soon vanished into the dark and all we could hear was the faint sound of its oars. Then, not even that. The breeze was fresher now and the boat rocked on the slight swell, forcing us to pay more attention to the rhythm of our rowing. At the halfway point the captain told us to change places, so that we would not be too tired by the time it came to boarding the ship. Pencho Bullas took my place and Mascarúa took that occupied by Cagafuego.

'Quiet now, and be careful,' said Alatriste.

We were very close to the galleon. I could see in more detail its dark solid bulk, its masts silhouetted against the night sky. The lantern on the quarterdeck indicated exactly where the stern was. There was another lantern illuminating the shrouds, the rigging and the bottom of the mainmast, and light filtered out from two of the gunports that had been left open. There was no one to be seen.

'Stop rowing!' Alatriste whispered urgently.

The men stopped, and the boat bobbed about on the swell. We were less than twenty yards from the ship's vast stern. The light from the lantern was reflected in the water, almost right under our noses. On the side nearest to us, a small rowing boat was moored, and a rope ladder dangled down into it.

'Prepare the grappling irons.'

From beneath the benches the men produced four grappling hooks with knotted ropes attached to them.

'Start rowing again, but very quietly and very slowly.'

We began to move, with the sailor steering us towards the rowing boat and the ladder. Thus we passed beneath the high black stern, seeking out the shadows where the light from the lantern did not reach. We were all looking up, holding our breath, afraid that a face might appear at any moment, followed swiftly by a warning shout and a hail of bullets or a cannonade. Finally, the oars were placed in the bottom of the boat, and we glided forward until we touched the side of the galleon next to the rowing boat and immediately beneath the ladder. The noise of that collision was, I thought, enough to have woken the entire bay, but no one inside cried out; there was no word of alarm. A shiver of tension ran through the boat as the men unwrapped their weapons and got ready to climb the ladder. I fastened the hooks on my buff coat. For a moment Captain Alatriste's face came very close to mine. I couldn't see his eyes but I knew he was looking at me.

'It's every man for himself now,' he said quietly.

I nodded, knowing that he could not see me nod. Then I felt his hand squeeze my shoulder, firmly but briefly. I looked up and swallowed hard. The deck was some five or six cubits above our heads.

'Up you go!' whispered the captain.

At last I could see his face lit by the distant light of the lantern, the hawk-like nose above his moustache as he began to scale the ladder, looking upward, his sword and dagger clinking at his waist. I followed without thinking and heard the other men, making no attempt to be quiet now, throw the grappling irons over the edge of the ship, where they clattered onto the deck and clunked into place as they attached to the gunwale. Now there was only the effort of climbing, the sense of haste, the almost painful tension that gripped muscles and stomach as I grasped the sides of the rope ladder and hauled myself up, step by step, feet slipping on the damp slimy planks that formed the hull of the ship.

'Mother of God!' someone said below me.

A cry of alarm rang out above our heads, and

when I looked up, I saw a face peering down at us, half-lit by the lantern. The expression on the man's face was one of horror, as if unable to believe his eyes as he watched us climbing towards him. He may have died still not quite believing them because Captain Alatriste, who had reached him by then, stuck his dagger in his throat right up to the hilt, and the man disappeared from view. Now more voices could be heard above, and the sound of people running about below decks. A few heads peeped cautiously out from the gunports and immediately drew back, shouting in Flemish. The captain's boots scuffed my cheek when he reached the top and jumped onto the deck. At that moment another face appeared over the edge, a little further off, on the quarter-deck; we saw a lit fuse then a flash, and a harquebus shot rang out; something very fast and hard ripped past us, ending in a squelch of pierced flesh and broken bones. Someone beside me, climbing up from the boat, fell backwards into the sea with a splash but without uttering a word.

'Go on! Keep going!' shouted the men behind me, driving each other.

Teeth gritted, head hunched right down between my shoulders, I climbed what remained of the ladder as quickly as possible, clambered over the edge, stepped onto the deck and immediately slipped in a huge puddle of blood. I got to my feet, sticky and stunned, leaning on the motionless body of the slain sailor, and behind me the bearded

224

face of Bartolo Cagafuego appeared over the edge, his eyes bulging with tension, his gap-toothed grimace made even fiercer by the enormous machete gripped between his few remaining teeth. We were standing at the foot of the mizzen mast next to the ladder that led up to the quarterdeck. More of our group had now reached the deck via the ropes secured by grappling hooks, and it was a miracle that the whole galleon wasn't awake to give us a warm welcome, what with that single harquebus shot and the racket made by sundry noises – the clatter of footsteps and the hiss of swords as they left their sheaths.

With my sword in my right hand and my dagger in my left, I looked wildly about in search of the enemy. And then I saw a whole horde of armed men swarming onto the deck from down below, and I saw that most were as blond and burly as the men I had known in Flanders, and that there were more of them to the stern and in the waist, between the quarterdeck and the forecastle, and I saw as well that there were far too many of them, and that Captain Alatriste was fighting like a madman to reach the quarterdeck. I rushed to help my master without waiting to see if Cagafuego and the others were following. I did so muttering the name of Angélica as a final prayer, and my last lucid thought, as I hurled myself into the fight with a furious howl, was that if Sebastián Copons did not arrive in time the *Niklaasbergen* adventure would be our last.

CHAPTER 9

OLD FRIENDS AND OLD ENEMIES

The hand and arm grow tired of killing too. Diego Alatriste would gladly have given what remained of his life – which was perhaps very little – to put down his weapons and lie quietly in a corner, just for a while. By that stage he was fighting out of a mixture of fatalism and habit, and his feeling of indifference as to the result may, paradoxically have been what kept him alive in the midst of all the clash and confusion. He was fighting with his usual serenity, without thinking, trusting in his keen eye and swift reactions. For men like him and in situations such as this one, the most effective way of keeping Fate at bay was to leave imagination aside and put one's trust in pure instinct.

Using his foot for leverage, he wrenched his sword from the body of the man he had just skewered. All around him there were shouts, curses and moans, and from time to time the gloom was lit up by a shot from a pistol or Flemish harquebus, offering a glimpse of groups of men furiously knifing each other and of puddles of blood that slithered into the scuppers as the ship tilted.

In the grip of a singular lucidity, Alatriste parried a thrust from a scimitar, dodged another, and responded by plunging his sword vainly into the void, yet he gave this error no thought. The other man drew back and turned his attention to someone else, who was attacking him from behind. Alatriste took advantage of that pause to lean against the bulkhead for a moment and rest. The steps to the quarterdeck stood before him, lit from above by a lantern; they appeared to be free, but he'd had to fight three men to get there; no one had warned him that there would be such a large company on board. The high poop deck, he thought, would provide a useful stronghold until Copons arrived with his men, but when Alatriste looked around, he found that most of his party were engaged in fighting for their lives and had barely moved from the spot where they had boarded.

He forgot about the quarterdeck and returned to the fray. He encountered someone's back, possibly that of the man who had escaped him before, and plunged his dagger into his opponent's kidneys, turning the blade so as to cause as much damage as possible, then yanking it out as the fellow dropped to the floor, screaming like a man condemned. A shot nearby dazzled him, and knowing that none of his men was carrying a pistol, he slashed his way blindly towards the source of the flash. He collided with someone, made a grab for him, but skidded and fell on the blood-washed deck, headbutting the other man in the face again and again until he could get a grip on his own dagger and slip it in between them. The Fleming screamed as he felt the knife go in and crawled away on all fours. Alatriste spun round, and a body fell on top of him, murmuring in Spanish, 'Holy Mother of God, Holy Mother of God.' He had no idea who the man was but had no time to find out. He pushed the body away and, sword in his right hand and dagger in his left, he scrambled to his feet with a sense that the darkness around him was turning red. The screams and shouting were truly horrendous, and it was impossible now to take more than three steps without slipping in blood.

Cling, clang. Everything seemed to be happening so slowly he was surprised that in between each thrust he made his adversaries did not dish out ten or twelve in return. He felt a hard blow to his cheek and his mouth filled with the familiar metallic taste of blood. He raised his sword up high in order to slash a nearby face – a whitish blur that vanished with a yelp. In the constant flux of battle Alatriste found himself back at the steps leading to the quarterdeck, where there was more light. He realised that he was still clutching under his arm a sword he had taken off someone although how long ago that had been, who could know? He dropped it and whirled round, dagger at the ready, sensing that there were enemies behind him, and at that moment, just as he was about to deal a counter-blow with his sword, he recognised the fierce bearded face of Bartolo Cagafuego, who was madly hitting out at anyone in his path, his lips flecked with foam. Alatriste turned in the other direction, seeking someone to fight, just in time to see a boarding-pike being propelled towards his face. He dodged, parried, thrust and then drove his sword in, bruising his fingers when the point of his blade stopped with a crunch as it hit bone. He stepped back to free his weapon and, as he did so, stumbled over some coiled cordage and fell so heavily against the ladder that he thought for a moment he had broken his spine. Now someone was trying to batter him with the butt of a harquebus, so he crouched down to protect his head. He collided with yet another man, whether friend or foe he could not tell; he hesitated, then stuck his knife in and drew it out again. His back hurt intensely, and he longed to cry out to gain some relief – emitting a long, half-suppressed moan was always a good way to take the edge off pain – but not a sound did he utter. His head was buzzing, he could still taste blood in his mouth, and his fingers were numb from gripping sword and dagger. For a moment he was filled with the desire to jump overboard. *I'm too old for this*, he thought desolately.

He paused long enough to catch his breath, then returned reluctantly to the fray. *This is where you die*, he said to himself. And at that precise moment, as he stood at the foot of the steps, encircled by the light from the lantern, someone shouted his name. Bewildered, Alatriste turned, sword at the ready. And he swallowed hard, scarcely able to believe his eyes. *May they crucify me on Golgotha,* he thought, *if it isn't Gualterio Malatesta.*

Pencho Bullas died at my side. The Murcian was caught up in a knife fight with a Flemish sailor when suddenly the latter shot him in the head at such close range that his head was ripped off at the jaw, spattering me with blood and brains. However, even before the Fleming had lowered his pistol, I had slit his throat with my sword, hard and fast, and the man fell on top of Bullas, gurgling something in his strange tongue. I whirled my sword about my head to fend off anyone attempting to close in on me. The steps up to the quarterdeck were too far away for me to reach and so I did what everyone else was attempting to do: I tried to keep myself alive long enough for Sebastián Copons to get us out of there. I didn't even have enough breath to utter the names of Angélica or Christ himself; I needed all the breath I had to save my own skin. For a while I managed to dodge whatever thrusts and blows came my way, returning as many as I could. Sometimes, amid the confusion of the fight, I thought I could see Captain Alatriste in the distance, but my efforts to reach him were in vain. We were separated by too many men killing and being killed.

Our comrades were putting on a brave face like

the practised swordsmen they were, fighting with the professional resolve of someone who has bet all his money on the joker, but there were far more men on board the galleon than we had expected, and they were gradually driving us back towards the gunwale over which we had boarded. *At least I can swim*, I thought. The deck was covered with motionless bodies or moaning figures dragging themselves along, causing us to stumble at every step. I started to feel afraid, not of death exactly – death is of no importance, Nicasio Ganzúa had said in the prison in Seville – but of shame, mutilation, defeat and failure.

Someone else attacked. He wasn't tall and blond like most of the Flemish, but sallow-skinned and bearded. He struck out at me, grasping his sword with both hands, but had little luck. I kept my head and stood firm, and the third or fourth time he drew back his arm I stuck my sword into his breast as swift as lightning, right up to the guard. My face almost touched his as I did so – I could feel his breath on mine – and we crashed to the floor together, with me still grasping the hilt, and I heard the blade of my sword snap as his back hit the deck. Then, for good measure, I stabbed him five or six times in the belly. At first I was surprised to hear him cry out in Spanish and for a moment thought I must have made a mistake and killed one of my own. However, the light from a lantern near the quarter-deck fell on an unfamiliar face. *So there are Spaniards on board too,*

I thought. Given the fellow's general appearance and the doublet he was wearing, he was clearly a professional swordsman.

I got to my feet, confused. This altered things, and not, by God, for the better. I tried to think what it could mean, but in the white heat of fighting there was no time to mull things over. I looked for some weapon other than my dagger and found a cutlass; it had a short broad blade, an enormous guard on the hilt and felt satisfyingly heavy in my hand. Unlike an ordinary sword, with its more subtle blade and sharp point to inflict penetrating wounds, the cutlass was excellent for slashing one's way through a throng. Which is what I did, *chaf, chaf,* impressed by the slick sound it made as I struck. I finished up next to a small group composed of the mulatto Campuzano, who continued to fight despite a great gash to his forehead, and El Caballero de Illescas, who was battling on exhausted and with little resolve, clearly seeking the first opportunity to hurl himself into the sea.

An enemy sword glittered before me. I raised the cutlass to deflect the blow and had barely completed that move when, with a sudden sense of panic, I realised my error. But it was too late. At that moment, near the small of my back, something sharp and metallic pierced my buff coat, entering the flesh. I shuddered to feel the steel slide sleekly between my ribs.

★   ★   ★

A fleeting thought went through Diego Alatriste's mind as he assumed the on-guard position. It all made sense: the gold, Luis de Alquézar, the presence of Gualterio Malatesta in Seville and here on board the Flemish galleon. The Italian was acting as escort to the cargo, which is why they had encountered such unexpectedly stiff resistance: most of the men they had been fighting were Spanish mercenaries like them, not sailors. In fact, this was a fight to the death between dogs of the same pack.

He had no time to think anything more because after the initial surprise – Malatesta seemed as taken aback as he – the Italian advanced on him, black and menacing, sword foremost. As if by magic, the captain's weariness vanished. There is no greater tonic to the humours than an ancient hatred, and his burned as brightly as ever. The desire to kill proved stronger than mere instinct. Alatriste moved faster than his adversary, for when it came to the first thrust, he was already on guard, deflecting it with one short sharp flick, sending Malatesta staggering backwards as the point of Alatriste's sword came within an inch of his face. When the captain bore down upon him, he noticed that the bastard wasn't even whistling his usual wretched little tune – *tirurí-ta-ta* – or anything else for that matter.

Before the Italian could recover, Alatriste moved in close, wielding his sword and jabbing with his knife so that Malatesta had no alternative but to continue backing away, looking for an opportunity to get in his first proper strike. They clashed fiercely right beneath the steps leading to the quarterdeck, and then, still fighting, travelled as far as the shrouds on the other side of the ship in hand-to-hand combat, wielding their daggers, the guards of their swords locked together. Then the Italian lost his balance when he collided with the cascabel on one of the bronze cannon positioned there; Alatriste savoured the look of fear in his enemy's eyes, turned sideways on, gave a left thrust and then a right, point and reverse, but as luck would have it, he performed that last slashing attack with the flat of his sword not the edge. This was enough to provoke a ferocious yelp of glee from Malatesta, who, sly as a snake, drove his dagger forward with such vigour that if a startled Alatriste had not jumped out of the way, he would have surrendered his soul there and then.

'Well, well,' murmured Malatesta, out of breath, 'what a small world.'

He still appeared surprised to find his old foe on board. For his part, the captain said nothing and merely waited for the next onslaught. They paused, studying each other, swords and daggers in hand, crouched and ready to join battle again. All around them the fighting continued, and Alatriste's men were still getting the worst of it. Malatesta glanced across at them.

'This time, Captain, you lose. You've bitten off more than you can chew.'

The Italian was smiling serenely, as black as the Fates themselves, the murky light from the lantern throwing into sharp relief the scars and pockmarks on his face.

'I hope,' he added, 'you haven't got the boy involved in this scrimmage.'

That was one of Malatesta's weak points, thought Alatriste as he made a downward thrust: he talked too much and thus opened up gaps in his defence. The point of his sword caught the Italian's left arm, forcing him to drop his dagger with an oath. The captain took immediate advantage of this gap and made such a fearsomely fast low thrust with his dagger that the blade broke when he missed and hit the cannon instead. For a moment he and Malatesta stood very close, almost embracing, looking at each other. They both swiftly drew back their swords to gain some space and tried to get their knife in before the other one did; then the captain, resting his free – badly bruised – hand on the cannon, gave the Italian a sly kick that sent him slamming into the gunwale and the shrouds. At that point, behind them, they heard loud shouts coming from the waist of the ship, and a renewed clatter of swords spread across the deck. Alatriste did not turn round, intent as he was on his enemy, but from the expression on the latter's face, suddenly grim and desperate, he could tell that Sebastián Copons must finally have boarded at the prow. As if to confirm this, the Italian opened his mouth and let out a stream of blasphemies in his mother tongue; something about *el cazzo di Cristo* and *la sporca Madonna*.

Pressing my hands to my wound, I managed to drag myself over to the gunwale, where I leaned against some coiled ropes. I unfastened my clothes to find out what damage had been done to my right side but could see nothing in the darkness. It hardly hurt at all, apart from the ribs bruised by the steel blade. I felt the blood running gently over my fingers, down my waist to my thighs and onto the already gore-soaked deck. *I must do something*, I thought, *or else die like a stuck pig*. This idea made me feel faint, and I took deep breaths of air, struggling to remain conscious; fainting was the surest way to bleed to death. All around me the struggle continued, and everyone was far too occupied for me to ask them for help; plus of course it might be an enemy who came to my aid, and an enemy would blithely slit my throat. So I decided to keep quiet and manage on my own. Sliding slowly down onto my good side, I poked a finger into the wound to find out how deep it was – only about two inches, I reckoned. My new buff coat had more than repaid the twenty escudos I gave for it. I could still breathe easily, which meant that my lung was presumably unharmed, but the blood continued to flow, and I was growing weaker by the minute. *I have to stop the flow*, I said to myself, *or order a mass for my soul right away*. Anywhere else a handful of earth would have been enough to clot the blood, but here there was nothing, not even a clean handkerchief. Somehow or other, I had kept my dagger with me, because it was there gripped between my legs. I cut off a section of my shirt tail and pushed it into the wound. This stung violently; indeed, it hurt so much that I had to bite my lip in order not to cry out.

I was beginning to lose consciousness. *I've done all I can*, I thought, trying to console myself before falling into the black hole that was opening up at my feet. I wasn't thinking about Angélica or anything. As I grew steadily weaker, I rested my head against the gunwale, and then it seemed to me that everything around me was moving. *It must be my head spinning*, I decided. But then I noticed that the noise of battle had abated and all the shouting and bedlam were happening further off, towards the waist of the ship and towards the prow. A few men ran past, jumping over me, almost kicking me in their haste to escape and plunge into the water. I heard splashes and cries of panic. I looked up bewildered. Someone had apparently climbed the mainmast and was cutting the gaskets, because the mainsail suddenly unfurled and dropped down, half-filled by the breeze. Then my mouth twisted into a foolish happy grimace intended as a smile, for I knew then that we had won, that the group boarding at the prow had managed to cut the anchor cable, and the galleon was now drifting in the night towards the sandbank of San Jacinto.

★   ★   ★

I hope I have what it takes and I don't give in, thought Diego Alatriste, steadying himself again and grasping his sword. *I hope this Sicilian dog has the decency not to ask for mercy, because I'm going to kill him anyway, and I don't want to do it when he's disarmed.* With that thought and spurred on by the urgent need to finish the business there and then and make no last-minute errors, Alatriste gathered together what strength he had and unleashed a series of furious thrusts, so fast and brutal that even the best fencer in the world would have been unable to riposte. Malatesta retreated, defending himself with difficulty, but he still had sufficient sangfroid, when the captain was delivering his final thrust, to make a high oblique slashing movement with his knife that missed the captain's face by a hair's breadth. This pause was enough for Malatesta to cast a rapid glance around him, to see how things stood on the deck and to realise that the galleon was drifting towards the shore.

'I was wrong, Alatriste. This time you win.'

He had barely finished speaking when the captain made a jab at his eye with the point of his sword, and the Italian ground his teeth and let out a scream, raising the back of his free hand to his cut face, which was now streaming with blood. Even then he showed great aplomb and managed to strike out furiously and blindly, almost piercing Alatriste's buff coat and forcing him to retreat a little.

'Oh, go to Hell,' muttered Malatesta. 'You and the gold.'

Then he hurled his sword at the captain, hoping to hit his face, scrambled onto the shrouds and leapt like a shadow into the darkness. Alatriste ran to the gunwale lashing the air with his blade, but all he could hear was a dull splash in the black waters. He stood there, stock still and exhausted, staring stupidly into the dark sea.

'Sorry I'm late, Diego,' said a voice behind him.

Sebastián Copons was at his side, breathing hard, his scarf still tied round his head and his sword in hand, his face covered in blood. Alatriste nodded, his thoughts still absent.

'Many losses?'

'About half.'

'And Íñigo?'

'Not too bad. A small wound to the chest . . . but no damage to the lung.'

Alatriste nodded again, and continued staring at the sinister black stain of the sea. Behind him he heard the triumphant shouts of his men and the screams of the last defenders of the *Niklaasbergen*, having their throats cut as they surrendered.

I felt better once I had staunched the flow of blood, and the strength returned to my legs. Sebastián Copons had put a makeshift bandage on my wound, and with the help of Bartolo Cagafuego I went to join the others at the foot of the quarterdeck steps. Various men were clearing the deck by throwing corpses overboard, plundering them first for any objects of value they might find. The bodies dropped into the sea with a macabre splash, and I never found out exactly how many of the ship's crew, Flemish and Spanish, died that night. Fifteen or twenty, possibly more. The others had jumped overboard during the fighting and were swimming or drowning in the wake left by the galleon, which was now heading for the sandbanks nudged along by a breeze from the north-east.

On the deck still slippery with blood lay our own dead. Those who had boarded at the stern had borne the brunt. There they lay, motionless, hair dishevelled, eyes open or closed, in the precise pose in which the Fates had struck: Sangonera, Mascarúa, El Caballero de Illescas and the Murcian Pencho Bullas. Guzmán Ramírez had been lost to the sea, and Andresito el de los Cincuenta was moaning softly as he lay huddled and dying next to a gun carriage, a doublet thrown over him to cover his spilled guts. Less badly wounded were Enríquez el Zurdo, the mulatto Campuzano and Saramago el Portugués. There was another corpse stretched out on deck, and I stared for a while in surprise at the unexpectedness of the sight: the accountant Olmedilla's eyes remained half open as if, right until the last moment, he had kept watch to ensure that his duty to those who paid his salary was duly carried out. He was paler than usual, his customary ill-tempered sneer fixed for ever beneath the mousy moustache as if he regretted not having had the time to set everything down in ink in a neat hand on the standard official document. The mask of death made him look more insignificant than usual, very still and very alone. I was told that he had boarded along with the group at the prow, clambering over ropes with touching ineptitude, lashing out blindly with a sword he barely knew how to use; and that he had died at once without a murmur of complaint, and all for some gold that was not his own, for a King he had glimpsed only occasionally and from afar who did not know his name and who would not even have spoken to him had he walked past him in a room.

When Alatriste saw me, he came over and gently touched the wound, then placed one hand on my shoulder. By the light of the lantern I could see that his eyes retained the same absorbed expression they had during the fighting, indifferent to everything around us.

'Pleased to see you, lad.'

But I knew this wasn't true. He might well feel pleased later on, when his pulse returned to normal and order was restored, but at that moment his words were hollow. His thoughts were still fixed on Gualterio Malatesta and on the galleon now drifting towards the sandbank of San Jacinto. He scarcely looked at our dead comrades and gave Olmedilla's body only the most cursory of glances. Nothing seemed to surprise him nor alter the fact that he was alive and still had things to do. He dispatched Juan Eslava to the leeward side to report on whether we had yet reached the sandbank or the shallows; he ordered Juan Jaqueta to make sure that no enemies remained hidden on board; and repeated the order that no one, for any reason, should go below. 'On pain of death,' he said sombrely, and Jaqueta, after looking at him hard, nodded. Then, accompanied by Sebastián Copons, Alatriste went down into the bowels of the ship. I would not have missed this for the world, and so I took advantage of my position as my master's page and followed behind, despite the pain from my wound, doing my best to make no sudden movements that might worsen the bleeding.

Copons was carrying a lantern and a pistol he'd picked up from the deck, and Alatriste had his sword unsheathed. We scoured every berth and hold but found no one – we saw a table set, the food untouched on the dozen or so plates – then finally we reached some steps that led down into the darkness. At the bottom was a door closed with a great iron bar and two padlocks. Copons handed me the lantern and went in search of a boarding-axe. It took only a few blows to break down the door. I held the lantern up to light the interior.

'God's teeth!' murmured Copons.

There was the gold and silver for which we had fought and killed. Stored away like ballast in the hold, the treasure was piled up in various barrels and boxes, all roped securely together. The ingots and bars lining the hold glowed like some extraordinary golden dream. In the distant mines of Peru and Mexico, far from the light of the sun, thousands of Indian slaves under the lash of the overseer had ruined their health and lost their lives in order that this precious metal should reach these shores, and all to repay the empire's debts, to finance the armies and the wars in which Spain was embroiled with half of Europe, to swell the fortunes of bankers, officials, unscrupulous aristocrats and, in this case, to line the pockets of the King himself. The gold bars glinted in Captain Alatriste's dark pupils and in Copons's wide eyes. And I watched, fascinated.

'What fools we are, Diego,' said Copons.

And there was no doubt about it: we were fools. I saw the captain slowly nod his agreement. We were fools not to hoist the sails – had we known how to do it – and to keep on sailing, not towards the sandbanks but out towards the open sea, into waters that bathed shores inhabited by free men, with no master, no god and no king.

'Holy Mother!' said a voice behind us.

We turned round. El Bravo de los Galeones and the sailor Suárez were standing on the steps staring at the treasure, slack-jawed with amazement. They were carrying their weapons in their hands and, over their shoulders, sacks into which they had been stashing anything of value they came across.

'What are you doing here?' asked Alatriste.

Anyone who knew him would have taken great care over their answer. El Bravo de los Galeones, however, did not. 'Just having a bit of a walk about,' he replied brazenly.

The captain smoothed his moustache, his eyes as hard and fixed as glass beads.

'I said no one was to come down here.'

'Yeah, well,' said El Bravo dismissively. He was smiling greedily, a fierce look on his scarred, face. 'And now we know why.'

He was gazing wildly at the glittering treasure. Then he exchanged a glance with Suárez, who had put his sack down on the steps and was scratching his head incredulously, stunned by what lay before him.

'It seems to me, comrade,' said El Bravo de los Galeones, 'that we should tell the others about this. That would be a fine tric—'

The word became a mere gurgle in his throat as Alatriste, without warning, stuck his sword through El Bravo's breast so quickly that by the time the ruffian had a chance to stare down in stupefaction at the wound, the blade had already been removed. Mouth agape and uttering an agonised sigh, El Bravo fell forward onto the captain, who pushed him away, leaving him to roll down the steps and land at the very foot of a barrel of silver. When he saw this, Suárez let out a horrified 'Dear God!' and instinctively raised the scimitar he was carrying; then he seemed to think better of it, for he turned on his heel and started

244

climbing back up the steps as fast as he could, stifling a scream of terror. And he continued to scream that muffled scream until Sebastián Copons, who had unsheathed his dagger, caught up with him, grabbed his foot and knocked him down; then, straddling his body, he yanked Suárez's head up by the hair and deftly cut his throat. I watched this scene frozen in horror. Not daring to move a muscle, I saw Alatriste wiping the gore from his sword on the prone body of El Bravo, whose blood was now soiling the gold ingots piled up on the floor. Then he did something strange: he spat as if he had something dirty in his mouth. He spat into the air as if he were making some comment to himself, or like someone uttering a silent oath, and when his eyes met mine I shuddered because he was looking at me as if he did not know me, and for an instant I was afraid he might kill me as well.

'Watch the stairs,' he said to Copons.

From where he was kneeling beside the inert corpse on which he was cleaning his dagger, Copons nodded. Then Alatriste walked past him without so much as a glance at the sailor's dead body and went back up on deck. I followed him, glad to leave behind me the awful scene in the hold, and, once aloft, I noticed that Alatriste had paused to take a deep breath, as if desperate for the air that had been lacking below. Then Juan Eslava shouted to us from the gunwale, and almost simultaneously we felt the keel of the ship grind into the sand. All movement ceased, and the deck listed slightly to one side. The men were pointing at lights moving on the shore, coming to meet us. The *Niklaasbergen* had run aground in the shallows of San Jacinto.

We went over to the gunwale. There were boats rowing towards us in the dark, and a line of lights was approaching slowly from the end of the spit of sand, where the water beneath the galleon looked bright and clear in the lantern light. Alatriste glanced at the deck.

'Right, let's go,' he said to Juan Jaqueta.

The latter hesitated for a moment.

'Where are Suárez and El Bravo?' he asked uneasily. 'I'm sorry, Captain, but I couldn't help it—' He suddenly paused, studying my master's face in the light near the quarterdeck. 'I'm sorry, but to stop them, I'd have had to kill them.'

He fell silent.

'Kill them,' he repeated in soft bewildered tones.

This sounded more like a question than a statement. But there was no reply.

Alatriste was still looking around him. 'It's time we left the ship,' he said, addressing the men on deck. 'Help the wounded off.'

Jaqueta was still watching him. He seemed to be waiting for an answer. 'What happened?' he asked grimly.

'They're not coming.'

The captain at last turned to face Jaqueta, coldly and calmly. Jaqueta opened his mouth but said nothing. He stood like that for a moment then turned to the other men, urging them to obey the captain's orders. The boats and lights were coming nearer, and our men began to climb down the rope ladder to the tongue of sand uncovered by the low tide on which the galleon had run aground. Bartolo Cagafuego and the mulatto Campuzano, whose head was swathed in a huge bandage like a turban, were carefully helping Enríquez el Zurdo off the ship; El Zurdo was bleeding profusely from a broken nose and had a couple of nasty cuts to his arms. Ginesillo el Lindo went to the aid of Saramago, who was limping painfully from a long gash in his thigh.

'Any closer and they'd have had my balls,' Saramago said mournfully.

The last to leave were Jaqueta – once he had closed the eyes of his comrade Sangonera – and Juan Eslava. No one had to bother with Andresito el de los Cincuenta because by then he had been dead for some time. Copons appeared at the top of the steps to the hold and went straight over to the side of the ship. At that moment a man climbed on board, and I recognised the fellow with the ginger moustache who had spoken to Olmedilla earlier. He was still dressed as a hunter and was armed to the teeth; behind him came several more men. Despite their disguise, they were all clearly soldiers. They eyed with professional curiosity the bodies of our dead comrades and the blood-stained deck, and the man with the ginger moustache stood for a while studying Olmedilla's corpse. Then he came over to the captain.

'How did it happen?' he asked, pointing to the accountant.

'As these things do,' said Alatriste laconically.

The other man looked at him intently, then said equally, 'Good work.'

Alatriste did not respond. Heavily armed men continued to clamber on board. Some were carrying harquebuses with the fuses lit.

'In the name of the King,' said the man with the ginger moustache, 'I take charge of this ship.'

I saw my master nod. Then I followed him over to the gunwale, where Sebastián Copons was already climbing down the rope ladder. Alatriste turned to me with that same distracted air and put a helping arm around me. I leaned against him and breathed in the smell of leather and steel mixed with the odour of blood from the men he had killed that night. He went down the ladder, all the while supporting me, until we reached the sand. The water came up to our ankles. We got wetter as we waded towards the beach, plunging in up to our waists, which made my wound sting fiercely. Shortly afterwards, with me still leaning on the captain for support, we reached land, where our men had gathered in the darkness. Around them were the shadows of more armed men as well as the blurred shapes of many mules and carts ready to carry off what lay in the ship's holds.

248

'Ye gods,' said one man, 'we certainly earned our keep tonight.'

These words, spoken in a cheery tone of voice, broke the silence and the tension. As always after combat – and I had seen this time and again in Flanders – the men gradually began to talk and open up, with just a comment here and there at first, brief remarks, complaints and sighs. Then they launched into oaths and boasts and laughter: I did this, someone else did that. Some described in detail how they had boarded the ship or else asked how such and such a comrade had died. I heard no one regret the passing of the accountant Olmedilla: they had never taken to the scrawny individual dressed all in black, and it was clear as day that he had been ill-equipped for such work. As far as everyone there was concerned, his life wasn't worth a candle.

'What happened to El Bravo de los Galeones?' asked someone. 'I didn't see him peg it.'

'No, he was alive at the end,' said another.

'Suárez didn't get off the ship either,' added a third.

No one gave an explanation, and those who had one kept quiet. There were a few muttered comments, but Suárez had no friends amongst the crew, most of whom also loathed El Bravo. No one really felt their absence.

'All the more for us, I suppose,' remarked one man.

Someone gave a coarse guffaw, and the subject

was dropped. And I wondered – and had few illusions about the answer – if I had been lying on deck, stiff and cold as a piece of salt tuna, would I have merited the same epitaph? I saw the silent shadow of Juan Jaqueta, and although I couldn't see his face I knew he was looking at Captain Alatriste.

We walked to a nearby inn which had been prepared to receive us for the night. The innkeeper – a scurvy knave if ever there was one – had only to witness our faces, our bandages and our ironware in order to treat us as diligently and obsequiously as if we were grandees of Spain. And so there was wine from Jerez and Sanlúcar for everyone, a fire to dry our clothes by and abundant food of which we ate every crumb, for the violent fracas had left all of us with empty bellies. Mugs of wine and plates of roast kid were quickly dispatched, and we drank to our dead comrades and to the gleaming gold coins piled up on the table before us; these had been delivered before dawn by the man with the ginger moustache, who came accompanied by a surgeon who was to attend to our injuries; he cleaned the wound in my side, sewed it up, applied some ointment and a fresh clean bandage. Gradually, amid the vinous vapours, the men all fell asleep. Occasionally, El Zurdo or Saramago would moan or there would be raucous snores from Copons, who was sleeping stretched out on a rug, as oblivious to his surroundings as he had been in the mud of the Flanders trenches.

Discomfort prevented me from sleeping. It was my first wound, and I would be lying if I said that the pain from it did not fill me with a new and inexpressible pride. Now, with the passing of time, I bear other such marks on both flesh and memory: that first wound is only a near-imperceptible line on my skin, tiny compared with the wound I suffered at Rocroi or the one inflicted on me by Angélica de Alquézar's dagger. But sometimes I run my fingers over it and remember, as if it were yesterday, that night at Barra de Sanlúcar, the fighting on board the *Niklaasbergen*, and El Bravo's blood staining the King's gold with red.

Nor can I forget Captain Alatriste as I saw him in the early hours of that morning when pain kept me from sleep. He was sitting on a stool apart from everyone else, his back against the wall, watching the grey dawn creep in through the window while he drank his wine slowly and methodically as I had so often seen him do before, until his eyes became like opaque glass, his head sank slowly onto his chest, and sleep – a lethargy not unlike death – overwhelmed both body and mind. And I had shared his life for long enough to know that, even in his dreams, Diego Alatriste would continue to move through the personal wilderness that was his life, silent, solitary and selfish, oblivious to everything except the clear-sighted indifference of one who knows the narrow line that separates being

251

alive from being dead, of one who kills in order to preserve his life's breath and to keep himself in hot meals. One who is reluctant to obey the rules of that strange game: the old ritual in which men like him have been immersed since the world began. Such things as hatred, passionate beliefs and flags had nothing to do with it. It would doubtless have been more bearable if, instead of the bitter clarity that filled his every act and thought, Captain Alatriste had enjoyed the magnificent gifts of stupidity, fanaticism or malice, because only the stupid, the fanatical and the malicious live lives free from ghosts or remorse.

EPILOGUE

The sergeant of the Spanish guard cut an imposing figure in his red and yellow uniform, and he eyed me with some irritation as I walked through the palace gates with Don Francisco de Quevedo and Captain Alatriste. He was the same burly moustachioed fellow with whom I'd had words several days before outside those very walls, and he was doubtless surprised to see me there in my new doublet, with my hair combed, and looking handsomer than Narcissus himself, while Don Francisco showed him the document authorising us to attend the royal reception being held in honour of the municipal council and commercial tribunal of Seville to celebrate the arrival of the treasure fleet. Other guests were arriving too: wealthy merchants accompanied by spouses decked out in jewels, mantillas and fans; minor aristocrats who had probably pawned their few remaining valuables in order to buy new clothes especially for the occasion; clerics in cassock and cloak; and representatives of the local guilds. Almost everyone was staring open-mouthed this way and that, overwhelmed and impressed by the splendid appearance of the Spanish, Burgundian and German guards, as if half-afraid that at any moment someone would demand to know what they were doing there and throw them out into the street. All the guests knew that they would see the King and Queen only for an instant and from a distance, that their contribution would consist of little more than doffing their hats and bowing low to Their august Majesties as they passed. However, the mere fact of being present at such an event and being able to stroll like grandees in all their finery in the gardens of that former Moorish palace and talk about it afterwards, this was the very acme of the ambitions cultivated by even the most plebeian of Spaniards. And when the following day this fourth Philip proposed, perhaps, that the municipal council should approve the imposition of a new charge or an extraordinary tax on the newly arrived treasure, he would do so in the knowledge that Seville still had enough of a taste of syrup in its mouth to sweeten that bitter pill – for the deadliest thrusts are always those that pierce the purse – and would therefore loosen its purse-strings without too much complaint.

'There's Guadalmedina,' said Don Francisco.

The Count, who was chatting to some ladies, saw us from afar, excused himself with a gracious bow and came to meet us, oozing politeness and wearing his very best smile.

'By God, Alatriste, you've no idea how pleased I am to see you.'

He greeted Quevedo with his usual bonhomie, complimented me on my new doublet and gave the captain a gentle friendly pat on the arm.

'There's someone else who's very pleased to see you too,' he added.

He was dressed as elegantly as ever, in pale blue with silver braiding and with a magnificent pheasant feather in his hat. His courtly appearance was in marked contrast to that of Quevedo, who was dressed all in black with the cross of St James on his breast, and of my master, dressed entirely in browns and blacks, in an old but clean and scrupulously brushed doublet, canvas breeches, boots and with a gleaming sword hanging from his newly polished belt. His only new acquisitions were his hat – a broad-brimmed felt affair with a red feather in it – the starched white Walloon collar which he wore open as befitted a soldier, and the dagger bought for ten escudos to replace the one he had broken during his encounter with Gualterio Malatesta, a magnificent blade nearly two spans long and bearing the marks of the swordsmith Juan de Orta.

'He didn't want to come,' said Don Francisco, indicating the captain.

'I imagined he wouldn't,' replied Guadalmedina. 'However, there are some orders that must be obeyed.' He winked familiarly. 'Certainly by a veteran like you, Alatriste. And this *is* an order.'

The captain said nothing. He was looking awkwardly about him, occasionally tugging at his clothes as if he didn't know quite what to do with his hands. Beside him, Guadalmedina stood smiling to this person or that, waving to an acquaintance, sometimes nodding to the wife of a merchant or pettifogging lawyer, who then furiously fanned away her blushes.

'I should tell you, Captain, that the parcel reached its addressee, and that everyone took great pleasure in it,' he said with a smile, then lowered his voice. 'Well, to be honest, some took rather less pleasure in it than others. The Duke of Medina Sidonia very nearly died of grief. And when Olivares returns to Madrid your friend the royal secretary Luis de Alquézar will certainly have some explaining to do.'

Guadalmedina continued chuckling to himself, vastly amused, all the while waving and nodding and generally flaunting his impeccably courtly appearance.

'The Count-Duke is in the seventh heaven of delight,' he went on, 'happier than if Christ himself had struck Richelieu down with a thunderbolt. That is why he wanted you to be here today, to greet you, albeit from a distance, when he passes by with the King and Queen. You can't deny that it's quite an honour to receive a personal invitation from the King's favourite.'

'Our captain,' said Quevedo, 'feels that the greatest honour the Count-Duke could have bestowed on him would have been simply to forget the whole affair.'

'He may be right,' commented the Count. 'The favour of the great is often both more dangerous and more paltry than being out of favour. I can only say that it's very fortunate that you're a soldier, Alatriste, because you would make a disastrous courtier. I wonder sometimes if my profession isn't harder than yours.'

'To each his own,' replied the captain.

'Quite. But returning to the matter in hand, I'll have you know that yesterday the King himself asked Olivares to tell him the story. I was there, and the Count-Duke painted a very vivid picture. As you know, Our Catholic Majesty is not one to show his feelings, but I'll be hanged if I didn't see him blink several times while he listened to the account, and for him that's the very height of emotion.'

'Will this translate into anything tangible?' asked Quevedo, ever practical.

'If you're referring to something that jingles and has a head and a tail, I doubt it. When it comes to cheese-paring, if Olivares pares it fine, then His Majesty pares it finer still. They consider that the work was paid for at the time, and very generously too.'

'True enough,' said Alatriste.

'Well, you would know,' said the Count with a shrug. 'Today is, shall we say, by way of an honorific coda. The King's curiosity was aroused when he was reminded of your involvement in that incident two years ago with the Prince of

Wales at the Corral del Príncipe. And so he has a fancy to see you in the flesh.' The Count paused significantly. 'The other night, at Triana, it was far too dark.'

He fell silent again, studying Alatriste's impassive face.

'Did you hear what I said?'

My master held his gaze but did not respond, as if the Count had spoken of something which he felt neither the need nor the desire to remember, something in which he preferred not to be implicated. After a moment the Count looked away, slowly shaking his head and smiling to himself. He understood. Then his eyes fell on me.

'They say the boy acquitted himself well,' he said, changing the subject. 'And that he even brought away with him a nice little souvenir.'

'Yes, he acquitted himself very well indeed,' agreed Alatriste, making me blush with pride.

'Regarding this afternoon, you know the protocol,' Guadalmedina said, indicating the large doors that opened out onto the garden. 'Their Majesties will enter through there, the yokels will bow, and then the King and Queen will leave through that door over there. It'll be over in a flash. As for you, Alatriste, all you have to do is doff your hat and, for once in your wretched life, bow that stubborn soldier's head of yours. The King – who will as usual be gazing at some point on the horizon – will merely glance at you for a moment. Olivares will do the same. You nod, and that's that.'

'What an honour,' said Quevedo ironically. And then, so softly that we had to lean closer to hear, he recited these lines:

'See them all decked out in purple,
Hands beringed with glittering gems?
Inside, they're nought but putrefaction,
Made of mud and earth and worms.'

Guadalmedina, very much the courtier that afternoon, started back. He looked around him, gesturing to Quevedo to restrain himself.

'Really, Don Francisco, a little decorum, please. This is hardly the time or the place. Besides, there are people who would cut off their right hand for one glance from the King.' He turned to the captain and, adopting a persuasive tone, said, 'Anyway, it's no bad thing that Olivares should remember you and invite you here. You have a number of enemies in Madrid, and it's quite a coup to be able to count the King's favourite among your friends. It's high time you shook off the poverty that's been dogging you like a shadow. And as you yourself once said to Don Gaspar – and in my presence too – one never knows.'

'It's true,' replied Alatriste. 'One never knows.'

There was a roll of drums on the far side of the courtyard followed by a short blast on a trumpet, at which all conversation stopped and fans ceased fluttering, a few hats were rapidly doffed, and everyone turned expectantly in the direction of the fountains, the neat hedges and the pleasant rose gardens. On the far side of the courtyard the King and Queen and their cortège had just emerged from a room full of lavish hangings and tapestries.

'I must go and join them,' said Guadalmedina. 'I'll see you later, Alatriste, and, if you can manage it, try to smile a little when the Count-Duke looks at you. No, on second thoughts, don't. A smile from you usually heralds an attack!'

He left, and we stayed where we were, on the very edge of the white path bisecting the garden, while people to either side of us moved away, eyes fixed on the slowly advancing procession. Ahead came two officers and four archers from the royal guard, and behind them the cream of the royal entourage, gentlemen- and ladies-in-waiting, the former dressed in fine costumes adorned with diamonds and gold chains, and wearing court swords with gilded hilts; the latter wearing shawls, plumed hats, jewels, lace and lavish dresses.

'There she is,' whispered Quevedo.

There was no need for him to say any more because I, struck dumb and rooted to the spot, had already seen her. Amongst the Queen's maids of honour was Angélica de Alquézar, her golden ringlets brushing the delicate near-transparent shawl drawn tight about her shoulders. She was as lovely as ever, with at her waist the interesting addition of a small jewel-encrusted silver pistol, which looked as if it could fire real bullets and which she wore like an ornament on the scarlet watered satin of her skirt. A Neapolitan fan hung from her wrist, but her head was unadorned apart from a delicate mother-of-pearl comb.

Then she saw me. Her blue eyes, which had until then been staring blankly ahead, suddenly focused on me as if she had sensed my presence or as if, by dint of some strange witchcraft, she had been expecting to find me on that precise spot. She gave me a long lingering look without glancing away or appearing in the least discomfited. And just as she was about to walk past me, which would mean, of course, that she could only maintain eye contact by turning her head, she smiled. And what a glorious smile it was, as bright as the sun gilding the battlements of the Reales Alcázares. Then she was gone, moving off along the path, and I was left standing there like a gaping fool, having entirely surrendered my three faculties – memory, understanding and will – to her love, and thinking that I would gladly have returned again and again to the Alameda de Hércules or to the *Niklaasbergen*, ready to offer up my life if only she would smile at me like that one more time. And so fast were my heart and pulse beating that I felt a sudden pang, a sudden warm dampness under the bandage, where my wound had just reopened.

'Ah, my boy,' murmured Don Francisco de

Quevedo, placing an affectionate hand on my shoulder. 'So it is and so it shall always be: you will die a thousand times and yet your griefs will never kill you.'

I sighed, incapable of saying a word. And I heard the poet softly reciting:

'The beautiful creature from behind her bars
Promises that she's mine, only mine.'

The King and Queen, in their slow stiff progress, had by then almost drawn level with us. The young blond Philip, strongly built and erect, his gaze fixed as ever on some point in the middle distance, was dressed in blue velvet trimmed with black and silver, and around his neck on a black ribbon and gold chain he wore the badge of the Order of the Golden Fleece. The Queen, Doña Isabel de Borbón, was wearing a silver-grey dress with orange taffeta cuffs, and a bejewelled and feathered hat that set off her sweet youthful face. Unlike her husband she smiled charmingly at everyone, and it was a delight to see that beautiful French-born Spanish queen, the daughter, sister and wife of kings, whose cheerful nature brightened the sombre Spanish Court for two decades and aroused certain sighs and passions about which I will perhaps tell you on another occasion. She refused outright to live in El Escorial – that dark sombre austere palace built by her husband's grandfather – but, in one of life's little ironies from which no one is exempt, the poor thing was finally obliged to take up permanent residence there when she was buried along with the other queens of Spain.

But on that festive afternoon in Seville such things were all a long way off. The King and Queen looked so young and elegant, and as they passed everyone removed their hats and bowed before Their royal Majesties. Accompanying them was the imposing burly figure of the Count-Duke of Olivares, the very image of power in his black clothes, with that mighty back of his which, like Atlas, bore the awful weight of the vast monarchy of Old and New Spain, an impossible task which years later Don Francisco de Quevedo summed up in three lines:

> *How much easier it is, O Spain,*
> *For everyone to steal from you alone*
> *What you alone stole from everyone.*

Don Gaspar de Guzmán, Count-Duke of Olivares and minister to our King, wore a broad Walloon collar and the cross of Calatrava embroidered on his breast; the fierce points of his vast moustache rose up almost as far as his wary, penetrating eyes, which shifted constantly, restlessly, back and forth – identifying, recording, recognising. The King and Queen stopped rarely and always at the Count-Duke's suggestion, and when this happened, the King or the Queen or both at once would gaze

263

upon some fortunate person who for whatever reason – because of services performed or through influential contacts – was deemed deserving of that honour. In such cases the women curtsied low to the floor and the men bowed from the waist, their hats already having been doffed; then, after the gift of this moment of contemplation and silence, the King and Queen would continue their solemn march. Behind them came select Spanish nobles and grandees, amongst them the Count of Guadalmedina; as he approached us, Alatriste and Quevedo, along with everyone else, removed their hats, and the Count dropped a few words into the ear of the Count-Duke, who bestowed on our group one of his fierce looks, as merciless as an indictment. The Count-Duke in turn whispered into the ear of the King, who stopped walking, brought his gaze down from the heights and fixed it on us. While the Count-Duke was still murmuring into his ear, the King, his prognathous bottom lip protruding, rested his faded blue eyes on Captain Alatriste.

'They're talking about you,' muttered Quevedo.

I glanced at the captain. He remained upright, his hat in one hand, his other hand resting on the hilt of his sword, with his stern moustachioed profile and serene soldierly head looking straight at the King, at the monarch whose name he had shouted out on battlefields and for whose gold he had risked life and limb only three nights before. I saw that the captain seemed unimpressed and unabashed.

All his awkwardness had vanished, and there remained only his frank dignified gaze, which held that of the King with the equanimity of one who owes nothing and expects nothing. I remembered the moment when the old Cartagena regiment had mutinied at Breda, and I had been tempted to join the rebels, and how when the ensigns were leaving the ranks in order not to be tainted by the revolt, Alatriste had grabbed me by the scruff of the neck and forced me to leave with them, uttering the words, 'Your King is your King.' It was there, in the courtyard of the Reales Alcázares in Seville, that I finally began to understand the meaning of that singular dogma which I had failed to understand at the time: the loyalty professed by Captain Alatriste was not to the fair-haired young man standing before him, not to His Catholic Majesty nor to the one true religion, and not to the idea that either of them represented on Earth, but to that one personal rule, chosen for want of anything better, which was all that remained from the shipwreck of more generalised, more enthusiastic ideas that had dissolved with the loss of innocence and youth. Regardless of what the rule was – right or wrong, logical or illogical, just or unjust, justifiable or not – the rule mattered to men like Diego Alatriste as a way of imposing some kind of order or structure on the apparent chaos of life. And thus, paradoxically, my master respectfully doffed his hat before his king not out of resignation or discipline but out of despair. After all, since there were no

265

old gods in whom one could trust, no great words that could be bandied about during combat, it was a salve to everyone's honour – or at least better than nothing – to have a king for whom one could fight and before whom one could doff one's hat, even if one did not believe in him. And so Captain Alatriste held firmly to that principle, just as, had he given his loyalty to someone else, he might have pushed his way through that very same throng and knifed the King to death without a thought for the consequences.

At that point something unusual happened to interrupt my thoughts. The Count-Duke of Olivares concluded his short report, and the monarch's usually impassive eyes now took on an expression of curiosity and remained fixed on the captain. Then our fourth Philip gave the very slightest of approving nods and, slowly raising his hand to his august breast, removed the gold chain he was wearing and handed it to the Count-Duke. The latter, smiling thoughtfully, weighed it in his hand for a moment and to the general amazement of all those present came towards us.

'His Majesty would like you to accept this chain,' he said.

He uttered these words in the stern arrogant tone that was so typical of him, piercing the captain with the two hard black points of his eyes, a smile still visible beneath his fierce moustache.

'Gold from the Indies,' he added with evident irony.

Alatriste turned pale. He stood stock still and stared at the Count-Duke uncomprehendingly.

Olivares was still proffering him the chain in his outstretched palm. 'Well, don't keep me waiting all day,' he snapped.

The captain finally seemed to come to. And once he had recovered his composure, he at last took the chain and, stammering a few words of gratitude, looked again at the King. The latter continued to observe the captain with some curiosity, while Olivares returned to his monarch's side; Guadalmedina stood beaming amongst the other astonished courtiers and the cortège prepared to move on. Then Captain Alatriste bowed his head respectfully, the King nodded, again almost imperceptibly, and the procession set off.

Proud of my master, I looked defiantly around me at all those inquisitive faces staring in astonishment at the captain and wondering who the Devil this fortunate man was, to whom the Count-Duke himself had presented a gift from the King. Don Francisco de Quevedo was chuckling delightedly to himself and clicking his fingers, muttering about the need to wet both his whistle and his words at Becerra's inn, where he must set down some lines that had just occurred to him:

If what I have I do not fear to lose,
Nor yet desire to have what I do not,
I'm safe from Fortune's wheel whate'er I choose,
Let plaintiff or defendant by my lot.

He recited these lines to us for our pleasure, as gleefully as he always did when he found a good rhyme, a good fight or a good mug of wine.

So to the last, dear Alatriste, keep
Alone, alone, until the final sleep.

As for the captain, he remained standing amongst the other guests, not moving an inch, his hat still grasped in his hand, watching the royal cortège process through the Alcázar gardens. And then to my surprise I saw a cloud pass over his face, as if what had just happened had, suddenly and symbolically, bound him far more tightly than he wished to be bound. The less a man owes, the freer he is, and according to the world view of my master – who was capable of killing for a doubloon or a word – there were things never written or spoken which he considered to be as binding as friendship, discipline or an oath. Beside me, Don Francisco de Quevedo continued improvising lines for his new sonnet, but I knew, or sensed, that the King's gift of a gold chain weighed on Captain Alatriste as heavily as if it had been made of iron.

EXTRACTS FROM SOME FINE POETRY WRITTEN BY VARIOUS WITS OF THIS CITY OF SEVILLE

Printed in the seventeenth century without a printer's mark, and preserved in the 'Count of Guadalmedina' section of the Archive and Library of the Dukes of Nuevo Extremo (Seville).

ATTRIBUTED TO
DON FRANCISCO DE QUEVEDO

THE LAST EVENING AND END OF THE
RUFFIAN NICASIO GANZÚA, WHO DIED IN
SEVILLE FROM A VERY BAD SORE THROAT
BROUGHT ON BY THE ROPE.

First Ballad

In old Seville town, in its dark lofty prison
The cream of the thieves are now gathered together.
They have come to this place for a grand celebration,
A banquet in aid of Nicasio Ganzúa,
For at dawn he'll be issued his very last passport.
And it's thus only right, in His Majesty's prison,
For a solemn event to be given due weight;
But because it's the King who is giving the orders
No time must be lost – tempus fugit, my friends.
Here they come, brothers all of the criminal class,
Yes, those who are paid by the sum of their sword
*   thrusts*
And all of them dressed in the deepest of mourning,
Though armed to the teeth with glistening steel
(The jailor meanwhile has his itchy palm greased

270

With the silvery glitter of pieces of eight).
How they praise to the skies the condemnèd man,
Though their praises are not of a sacred kind,
See them sit round a table – the flower of ruffians –
For no honest rogue would ever dare miss
This wake for a man, for a hero illustrious.
How peacock-proud are these would-be nobles
(To be sure, in this gathering no women are found)
With their hats pulled down low o'er their faces, like
  grandees,
As they drink down whole mugs of the reddest of
  wines
And toast, with huzzahs, the health of Saint Glug,
For to men of the world he's their patron saint.
All drink to the fame of the bravest of comrades
Who, to judge by the barrel of wine they imbibe,
Must indeed be a man most worthy of honour.
At the fore is the handsome young Ginés el Lindo
Who, they say, is a practising doctor of fencing,
Even though he's a queer and strums the guitar.
Nearby, Saramago, that fine Portuguese,
Who's always prepared to spout some philosophy;
For sure, he's a doctor in utriusque
And wields with a flourish both a pen and a sword.
Another fine rogue can be seen paying court,
(From the town of Chipiona and sharp as a tack)
By name, El Bravo de los Galeones.
Then, Guzmán Ramírez, a man of few words,
Grabs a new deck of cards and is ready to play
With Rojo Carmona, his companion at table,
Who's known as a notable trickster to boot.

271

Many others there are in the thievery line,
Who love to distraction the pockets of others;
A newcomer there is, Diego Alatriste,
Who has come like a brother to be with Ganzúa.
And sitting beside him there's Íñigo Balboa,
A young man who showed at the great Siege of Breda
His courage in fighting – no coward was he.
While they're singing their songs and playing at cards,
While they carry on drinking the wine red as blood,
They are keeping a courteous eye on Ganzúa,
(For that is the least decent people can do)
Come when they're needed, give care without stint,
For such a misfortune may one day be theirs.

Second Ballad

They were deep in their game and their serious
    drinking
When the scribe with the guards came to read out
    the sentence
And all for the card-playing prisoner's sake.
But no interest he showed in these sonorous words,
Though his life's blood – so precious – depended on
    them;
More concerned was he then with the scoring of points.
When the scribe and the guard were about to depart,
A monk Augustinian offered confession,
Which was straightway declined by Nicasio Ganzúa.
Thus he turned down the chance to sing out at vespers
The tune that he never had warbled at prime.
When the monk and the officers finally left,

And Ganzúa was carefully playing his hand,
He found at the end that he held a trump card
And so won the game and collected his winnings.
Then, dealing again, he smoothed his moustache,
And in tones low and grave he addressed his confrères:
'I am helpless, my friends, I am stuck in this prison,
Till my neck is caressed by the rope in the morning
With a love so intense it will certainly kill me,
For I'll never escape its tight'ning embrace.
So allow me, my friends, a list of farewells,
My last will and testament, mark every word!
Were it not for the stool-pipe who sang out too loudly
I'd be free and not stupidly facing my death.
I ask you, friends all, give that slimiest of squealers
A good length of steel through the throat – make
  him bleed –
For to leave him the freedom to wag his long tongue
Is a curse and a plague and as deadly as sin.
Item Two: if you please, give a fistful of wishes
To the one who betrayed me – that traitorous
  jeweller –
Hit him hard in the chops when you give him my
  greetings,
For he certainly played me the vilest of tricks –
Thus make sure he will always remember my name.
Item Three: stick your knives several times in that
  catchpole,
That turd Mojarrilla, who handled me roughly
When I was arrested. And as for the judge
With his hand-me-down robe and his high noble
  ways,

273

Just give him the same, make him bleed for his
  pains.
And lastly, my whore, Maripizca,
Of clean blood and habits, my friends, look to her,
For though she's no child, proper "ladies" like her
Should not be alone when they walk down the
  street.
I close on this hour, on this date, in this place,
The very last will of the ruffian Ganzúa.'
Every heart there was moved and everyone stood
And did swear and did promise, as trusty friends
  should,
To execute, faithfully, all of his wishes.

Third Ballad

Ganzúa, awaiting his execution,
Was dressed in the finest of clothes,
He had never before looked so handsome as then
On the night all his friends sat with him.
He was wearing a doublet of fine purple cloth
Whose full sleeves were slashed à la mode,
And green canvas breeches that were held up in
  style
By a belt that was four inches wide,
And shoes for a light Sunday promenade,
Adorned with two bright scarlet bows,
Each shoe with a silvery buckle that glittered
Against the deep black of the leather.
Early next morning, to enter the square,
He changed to a simple serge gown

As befitting a man who was soon to be led
To the scaffold's bare high wooden hill –
Quite unlike the brave judges who put on their
  gowns
But stay safe and sound in their court.
He rode from the prison upon a grey mule,
Town crier stepping before
And carrying a cross and municipal rod
While he listed the prisoner's crimes.
Handsome Ganzúa rode on without falter,
(No trace of last night's carousing)
And greeted with courtly politeness and grace
All those he had known, great and small.
He looked quite serene, like a priest in procession,
So that one almost envied his fate.
No stumble he made as he climbed up the steps,
Though one step was broken and gaping.
And when he was standing at last on the boards
He turned to the crowd and spoke thus:
'Death is of little importance, my friends,
But since by the King it arrives,
Let no one deny the evident truth
That mine is an honourable one.'
All nodded and gravely accepted his words,
His whore and executors too.
And they thought it was equally proper and right
That his dear Maripizca had hired
A chorus of blindmen to sing for his soul.
A sermon then followed their prayers,
And he recited the Creed with no hint of a tremor,
For it's always a dreadful and shameful dishonour

275

When infamous ruffians break down and blubber.
The fell executioner stepped up behind
And placing the noose round the prisoner's neck
Said these words: 'O, my brother, I ask your
    forgiveness,'
Then quickly he tightened the noose until death.
Our brave Ganzúa did not flinch or grimace,
For death to him was as naught,
But with quiet indifference he bore himself
As though he were sunk deep in thought.

FROM THE SAME

ADVICE ADDRESSED TO CAPTAIN DIEGO ALATRISTE

Sonnet

If what I have I do not fear to lose,
Nor yet desire to have what I do not,
I'm safe from Fortune's wheel whate'er I choose,
Let plaintiff or defendant be my lot.

For if I joy not in another's pain
And worldly wealth brings me no hint of pleasure,
Grim death may come and take me without strain;
I'll not resist or ask for lesser measure.

And you, who even now know not the chains
With which this age imprisons a heart,
Diego – free from pleasures and from pains –
Keep, thus, far hence the prick of passion's dart;

So to the last, dear Alatriste, keep
Alone, alone, until the final sleep.

TRANSLATOR'S
ACKNOWLEDGEMENTS

I would like to thank Arturo Pérez-Reverte, Annella McDermott and Palmira Sullivan for all their help and advice, and give a special thank you to Ben Sherriff for his ever-willing assistance in translating the poetry.